THE NAMES IN THE HAT

The best lack all conviction, while the worst
Are full of passionate intensity.
                    —William Butler Yeats, "The Second Coming"

—

"Time evolves and comes to a place where it renews again.
There is first a purification time and then a renewal time.
We are getting very close to this time now."
                    —Elders Speak, Part 1 (YouTube)

TABLE OF CONTENTS

DEDICATION

To my favorite grandchildren, Eliza and Owen, and
to Frankie and the next seven generations.

THE LEGEND OF SLEEPING BEAR

Legend has it that many years ago, in Wisconsin, a mother bear lovingly raised her two cubs on the western shore of Lake Michigan. When a vast forest fire threatened to destroy everything in its path, the mother bear looked desperately across the Great Lake to Michigan and set out with her cubs to swim across the lake to the distant land.

After hours of swimming, the cubs grew more and more exhausted. Within sight of the Michigan shore, they could swim no longer. The mother bear was heartbroken as she watched them both drown.

Weary and sad, she came ashore and lay atop a high bluff, where she could look westward to where her cubs had been lost. As she kept watch over their watery grave, through a miracle of the Great Spirit Gitche Manitou, two beautiful islands emerged to mark where her cubs had vanished.

PART ONE

CHAPTER I

Pure Michigan

Even though his wife, Jacquie, was asleep in the passenger seat next to him, U.S Congressman Charlie Birnbaum couldn't stop from laughing out loud when he saw the blue-and-white sign emerging from the fog as they crossed the state line from Ohio into Michigan. "Pure Michigan" it said.

It was a happy laugh because he was glad to be back in his beautiful home state—and it was a rueful laugh, with full awareness of the turmoil and sadness affecting people's lives, and also, the problems and questions facing *him*. Charlie regularly flew home on weekends to meet with his constituents and to tend to local-office matters. Today, Jacquie and he were driving home for the 2017 Thanksgiving recess.

Opening her pale-blue eyes wide in surprise at being awakened, she said, "What is it this time?" Charlie laughed even more, causing Jacquie to smile in resignation. She sat up and brushed back her gray-streaked blonde hair. "Oh, my god. Look at the fog. How long have we been driving in this? Shouldn't we just pull over? So, what in the world are you laughing at, you old fool?"

"Oh, boy, just everything. Everything is so damned funny. That sign ... "

"Sign? What sign?"

"The Pure Michigan sign."

"I guess I missed it. But what's the big deal? That's been the state ad campaign for years now."

"Yeah, but just think about it for a minute."

"Charlie, dear, it's just an ad. It's a PR campaign, for goodness sakes. Better than 'Come to Flint and drink water laced with lead'."

"Actually, it's a beautiful campaign, and it's basically true, but sometimes it just hits me funny is all. And then, this fog. I had to laugh. Don't worry. I'm taking my time. We just ran into the fog a few minutes ago, after we left Toledo. I'm sure it will lift soon. But it makes me laugh. Remember yesterday, when we left D.C.?"

"Fog."

"Fog. Couldn't see the Monument. The radio said the White House was shrouded in gray. Then it lifted almost as soon as we got out of town—and here we are again. Welcome to Pure Michigan. Coincidence, I'm sure, but I just had to laugh—or I might just cry."

"As if," she said, and laughed along with him.

They laughed together a lot. It was one of their things. And talk. They talked with each other a lot. More than most couples that had been together over forty years.

In his early sixties, Charlie was still a young boy in many ways; even though many people considered him to be somewhat of a curmudgeon. His once long mop of straight yellow hair had turned into a long mop of stark-white, but in his eyes, he was still "The Blonde

Comet," the nickname a local newspaper caption writer had placed under the photo of Charlie winning the high-school state championship in the high hurdles. His friends had teased him unmercifully over the nickname. Eventually, it was shortened to "Comet," where it settled and stuck. A three-sport star—receiver in football, 6'3" forward in basketball (less now by an inch or two)—he engaged in each sport determined to win.

If there was anything Charlie loved more than competition, it was life itself. When he met someone new, in addition to a genuine winning smile and a handshake, he often made a joke. Then he would laugh at himself as if he just couldn't contain his pleasure at making a new friend. Like Will Rogers, he never met a person he didn't like. Most of all, perhaps, he loved kids—not just his three biological children with Jacquie, but also their two adopted children—a son from Guatemala and a daughter from Sudan—and their dozen or so grandchildren—but *all* kids. He had worked his way through Yale Law School; pursued a lifetime of work in local, state, and national politics; yet, kept his love of childlike play. Nothing had ever worn on him more than the troubles his home district of Flint Township had experienced over the last few years. Certainly, the inevitable ups and downs aged him, tempered him around the edges, and might have made him seem dour to others, and nobody but Charlie would consider him a comet anymore—but the little boy was still there, as was the competitor.

"Pure Michigan, my ass," he said. "Remember, after the lead-contamination problems started up? Ev Stenhouse blew it, blew it. Tone deaf."

3

Again, he rehashed the uproar across the state: the battle of the bands on the statehouse lawn—from Motown icons to Eminem and little-known folk-rock bands on the one side to Kid Rock and Ted Nugent on the other. The folk band created a new song—"WTF"—which Aretha Franklin turned into an anthem, giving rise not only to a campaign-rally theme but to a new political party: the WTF Party.

Jacquie laughed again and added the names of some of the other new political parties that had sprung up: the Good Times Party and the Party Party. "Their motto was 'let's just have some fun,'" she said.

"But the Peer Progressive Party had some good ideas," Charlie said.

Birnbaum saw Flint at the eye of a swirling storm that reached throughout the state of Michigan and even across the nation—amplified by a storm surge of turbulence, disorder, and disruption driven by breakdowns in health, safety, schools, economic conditions, and general infrastructure. No one trusted the state government's ability to govern.

Then William "Billy the Boy King" Boykin was elected President of the United states. The chaos of his first year in office only magnified the cataclysmic forces within Michigan. Fair or not, Charlie thought, Governor Everett Stenhouse was the face of it all.

Jacquie and he had watched the network news from their Reston, Virginia, apartment as people eventually surrounded the state Capitol in Lansing. The crowd loudly banged on pots and pans to drive the state officials who were trying to conduct business inside, including

Stenhouse, to the brink. Despite efforts of police to stop them, men and women scaled a wall of the Capitol and posted a banner that said: "Murder due to carelessness is still murder."

In the spring of 2017, both houses of the state Legislature, in desperation, simply adjourned and went home. By July, President Boykin, with massive troubles of his own making, bailed the governor out by bringing Stenhouse to Washington as the new Clean Water Czar.

"Clean Water Czar," Charlie said to Jacquie. "That was a good one."

"'*He'll be a terrific czar*,'" Jacquie said, quoting Boykin's tweet.

Before being thrust into the governor's chair as next in the line of succession, the Lieutenant Governor resigned. The Secretary of state took the job but made it clear she was only keeping the chair warm until the fall election of 2018—and she would not have anything to do with running for office ever again.

"Pure Michigan," Charlie repeated. "Sometimes you have to laugh or it'll drive you crazy. That sign in the fog just hit me."

"So, what do you *really* think, Charlie? You going to run?"

He paused a few beats. There was no better time in history for Charlie Birnbaum's comet to blaze again. The people of Michigan, as well as the people of the country, were demanding a fresh start—and Charlie had always broken fast out of the starting blocks.

The fog lifted as they neared Ann Arbor.

"I need to call Lana Hartman," Charlie finally answered. A former Republican Senate aide, Hartman now taught at the University of Michigan Law School.

"If you're going to run, of course you do," said Jacquie. "I take it then, that you've made up your mind."

"Maybe. Maybe not. But she can help me decide."

CHAPTER 2

Engadine Line 5

Only Angelo RoundSky and Garfield Township Police Captain Dan Jankowski were left behind to oversee the truce. They sat near each other on beach chairs, on opposite sides of the police tape that surrounded the pumping station. A short distance away, two reporters remained, one from the local weekly and the other from a downstate television station. The reporters paid little attention to the principals or to each other, spending much of their time trying to find a signal for their cellphones. Occasionally they paused to gossip or laugh at something. Expectations were low all around—not much was likely to happen.

The protest at Standing Rock, in the Dakotas, was growing by the day. In Michigan's Upper Peninsula, similar but smaller protests over the potential for leaks in Enbridge Line 5, a pipeline that crossed the UP from Wisconsin and included a five-mile stretch that ran under the Straits of Mackinac, had been ongoing for some time. The concern was that someday a spill springing from under the deep waters of the Straits would result in a freshwater disaster, something that could impact the entire Great Lakes region.

The major protest sites were centered near the "Mighty Mac" bridge that spanned the five miles from the Lower to the Upper Peninsulas. Smaller protest groups had also set up at a few spots along the line. The first of these small groups was in the village of Engadine, in Garfield Township, forty odd miles from the center of the action.

The township police—a captain and four constables—plus a couple Enbridge security guards, had taken turns standing watch over the small band of Water Protectors that had been gathered, without much fuss, for weeks. "The Engadine Standoff," locals joked. But it was Thanksgiving weekend and, like the famous Christmas truce between the Germans and the allies in World War I, the protesters and the police declared a temporary truce so they could be home with their families. Since it was also deer-hunting season, with just enough snow on the ground to make for good tracking, they decided the truce should be extended for the entire holiday weekend.

All morning, RoundSky and Jankowski didn't say a word to each other. RoundSky, a tall, athletic man of thirty, with long, shiny, black hair (sometimes worn in a single braid down his back), drank coffee and listened to a playlist on his iPhone. Jankowski, also a big man, but in his late fifties and considerably rounder in the belly, read an Elmore Leonard paperback and drank coffee. Both were interrupted from time to time by phone calls from their respective groups or their families, dropped signals often cutting the conversations short. Occasionally one or the other would stand and stretch, or pace, or go to their separate porta johns to relieve themselves of all that coffee.

About noon, the captain finally spoke. "I'm going over to Hannah's."

"Don't suppose you want me to come along?"

"How would that look, you think?"

"Probably messed up. Those two reporters would tag along and my people would hear about it and probably not like it."

"Same here."

Jankowski got up from his folding chair, tucked his book in his back pants pocket and headed for his car to drive the few hundred feet to Hannah's White Tail Diner, or, as the locals called it "The Engadine Dine and Whine"—the only restaurant in the small town.

After listening to his music a while longer, Angelo took out his cellphone and checked for a signal. Nothing. "The hell with it," he said to himself. He stood up, got in his truck, and drove to the cafe without waiting for Jankowski to return. Angelo usually walked the short distance but today he had his reasons. As he entered the diner, Hannah nodded toward the back. He passed through the bar, past the pool table and the foosball table. Jankowski was sitting in a room by himself, looking down at his open book on the table beside a bottle of PBR.

"Thought you might be comin'. Boring out there. Sit if you want. I haven't got my food yet."

"Sure?"

"Hannah won't let those media guys get to us back here. A man's gotta eat, eh?"

Angelo laughed to himself when the captain said "media." Seemed a bit grandiose.

Just then Hannah looked in. "No daily special for you,

right Chief? You want your cheeseburger rare and your French fries well done."

Angelo smiled. "You got it. But like I told you, I'm not ..."

"Yeah, I know. You're not a chief. Sorry, about that. Arnold Palmer, heavy on the tea?"

Angelo nodded.

Hannah delivered Jankowski's hot turkey sandwich with gravy and mashed potatoes. "Yours'll be right up, Chief," she said.

"No pastie today, Captain?" said Angelo.

"Naw, Thanksgiving and all."

The captain bowed his head for a few seconds and crossed himself. "You believe in God?" he asked Angelo.

"We have our gods, including a creator," said Angelo. "Different than yours though. Your god is up there some-place, right? In full charge all the time?"

"That's what they tell me."

"We're more horizontal, you might say. Gods all around us, and more like brothers and sisters, not in charge." He gestured his arm around the room.

"I don't buy *all* my church's hocus-pocus—but I *am* a Catholic Polak, so I pretty much go with the whole thing."

"Us *Injuns* have our beliefs, which you *Polaks* call superstitions. The same deal goes for you Polacks, only in reverse."

"Just be careful when you say Polak, eh?"

"Long as you don't call me a redskin."

"Not Indian either, I guess."

"We use Indian a lot ourselves. Probably shouldn't but we do."

"Native American?"

Angelo gazed off at the buck head mounted on the wall for a moment, then he turned to look directly into the captain's eyes. "Native," he replied. "Just native."

When Angelo's burger arrived, Jankowski said, "I don't always say grace before meals. But being it's Thanksgiving and all, I figured I should. My wife, Jeannie, she'll ask me later if I said grace, and I better be able to say yes."

"I have one of those myself."

"I've seen her out there. She looks to be a good, strong ... woman, eh?"

Angelo suspected Jankowski had been about to say squaw. "Her name is Lexi. She's not my wife, at least, not yet. But yes, she is strong. She's a manager at a cherry co-op. A good woman. Just got home from Standing Rock."

"She was in the big leagues, then." Jankowski paused. "So, anyway, I don't get your sideways gods, or whatever."

"It's not anything you need to understand. Our spirits don't command us. They advise us. We make up our own minds. Nobody or nothing can tell us what to do."

"I noticed, eh?" said Jankowski.

"Yeah, no doubt. It's got me in trouble more than once. Getting a little better at it, maybe. So, I guess you're a real Yooper?"

"Yep, raised nearby, in Watersmeet."

"Nimrod Nation. I saw that TV series about their basketball team."

"Every boy in Watersmeet has to play basketball. My team wasn't as good as that one though. They play on your reservation, down below?"

"Sure, some. I was a hockey player."

11

"I didn't know Indians played hockey."

Play it? We invented it. Called it 'shinny' back then. I was a leading goal scorer at every level, from peewee up through juniors, and then I played downstate on a traveling team. Hockey got me a scholarship into college."

"Oh, yeah. I think I remember reading about you, eh? You played up here, at Lake Superior State."

"Lasted almost a year, yeah. Coach recruited me hard but when I got there, he tried to turn me into the team goon. That's what an Indian player was supposed to do— be the enforcer not the scorer." He signaled Hannah for the check. "Like I said, I don't much like people to tell me what to do when it runs against what I want to do; so we parted ways." In truth, Angelo had found he liked beating up players on the other teams, and that scared him. He was afraid he was becoming that person.

"Too bad, eh?"

"Yeah, but I did learn what lose-lose means. I try not to do that anymore if I don't have to. To me, this whole country seems headed for lose-lose right now. People going batshit."

Jankowski sopped up the gravy from his plate with a piece of white bread and sat back.

"Not just here," Angelo continued. "I'm talking about protests all over the country about the campaign and the election a couple weeks ago."

"It's a democracy. One side wins, the other side loses."

"You call it a democracy. We call it 'rich white men rule.' Either way, read the papers: people in the streets, some getting shot at or shooting at somebody. Kids bullied in schools by kids who think Boykin's election makes it okay. A busload of nine- and ten-year-old kids from my rez rode about an hour and a half to see a hockey game over in Kalkaska. During the third period, some of the spectators started pouring beer on the kids and telling them to go back to their rez, and stuff like that. That kinda stuff has been going on for years, but it's even worse now."

"That right? Well, that's not what it's like around here. Till now, maybe. Not when I was growing up."

"Never in Watersmeet? Never in Engadine, right?

"Far as I know, anyway," Jankowski said as he rose to leave.

"See you, captain. I got your lunch."

"No need—plus, somebody might get the wrong idea, eh?"

"Too late. All taken care of. See you back on the job."

"Back on the job then," Jankowski said, shoving his book back into his pocket. "And, that stuff in Kalkaska? That's just plain wrong."

Angelo followed soon after. Nobody else in the place except the two reporters playing foosball, their baskets of nachos on the bar.

"Bye, Chief. Happy Thanksgiving," Hannah said.

"It's our day of mourning, Hannah."

He didn't drive straight back to the Engadine site. Instead, Angelo drove the six miles to the harbor at Naub-inway ("Place of Echos"), the northernmost point of Lake Michigan. The Anishnabik Apakkwasun (People's Lodge) showed no signs of life, so he continued on to the marina. He walked slowly out on the harbor's pier— there was only one fishing boat in a slip—and tried to see south to the Manitou Islands and Sleeping Bear Dunes, near where he had grown up and where Lexi was now. He knew it was too far off to see but looked anyway. When he was a kid, he did his best to see from Sleeping Bear Dunes across the 100 miles or so west to Wisconsin. He could see her cubs, the Manitous. On North Manitou, he had done his three-day fasting retreat as a teenager, trying to make contact with his personal Gitche Manitou. All he could see today was the expansive beauty of the lake— flat and calm on this cloudy, windless day—and the small Naubinway Island Light, not nearly as impressive as the Crib lighthouse near the Manitous.

He checked his phone again for a signal and found an email from Lexi.

> Ang,
> I am back home now and will be coming up to Engadine soon. I haven't had much time to reflect on my short time at Standing Rock. There were just so many feelings. Anger, sadness, happiness, empowerment, disbelief, belief.
>
> On my first morning there I woke up and was alone in the tent. I heard that a water ceremony and morning prayer were taking place so I changed into my warm clothes and went to look for the people.
>
> I heard my lodge Auntie speaking, then sharing our water songs with the people. As she sang, I watched as people lined up one by one to walk out on a makeshift altar that reached out into

the water. A man standing there helped them to the altar, and they knelt, offered tobacco and prayed. Then a different tribe doing their water song. Between songs, the crowd would chant "Water is life!" three times. Then they'd say it in Lakota. Then Spanish.

I started crying. I walked to the riverbank, knelt, put my hands on the frozen water, and said my prayers and let a few tears drop onto it.

You see, we wake up and immediately go into ceremony and pray for the protection of the water. But what do you think those soulless men of Morton County, SD, do when they wake up? I bet it's not to pray. They're so lost and I feel so bad for them. But I'm thankful beyond words that I was able to participate in that beautiful water ceremony that morning. I missed you. I wanted you there with me.

Love, Lex

The message only made Angelo more homesick. He was about to head back to his truck when he impulsively clambered up a pile of gigantic limestone boulders that made the breakwater. He wanted one more look. He sat down, looked toward the south again and the lighthouse. He thought about escape, just driving to his camp at Blue River. Nobody would give a damn or even notice. He stood up on the rocks. But what if? What would a major oil spill do to the lake? Someone needed to be here. Maybe he wasn't helping much, but still.

On his way back to Engadine, he decided he would buy a piece of whitefish at the dock later and bake it in some foil on his camp stove that evening. Maybe some of his Ojibwe brothers, the non locals who were also camping there, would be back from hunting and he could join them in a few beers while he listened to their hunting stories and lies. For now, he was headed back to his beach chair.

As Angelo sat down, Jankowski looked up from his paperback. "Thanks again for the lunch, eh?" Then he turned back to his book.

"No problem," Angelo replied, and put on his earphones.

The next morning, Jankowski showed Angelo the front-page story in the *St. Ignace News* about "closed-door settlement talks in the Engadine conflict" They both had a laugh at that. Lunch had evolved into a summit talk. Later, in Hannah's for lunch, Jankowski saw the two reporters playing foosball in the bar. While he ate, he read the scrawl under the noon newscast on Channel 4 from Traverse City: "Thanksgiving Pow-Wow on Engadine Standoff."

Maybe they know something we don't, he thought. In fact, maybe they got it right. He could only hope.

As far as he ever knew, the story didn't get picked up by any other media outlets.

CHAPTER 3

Manitou

In December, Line 5 was still very much a live issue, but Angelo and Captain Jankowski agreed it wasn't worth the effort to continue patrolling the Engadine portion of the line. It was so close to the main site in St. Ignace, it could be sufficiently monitored from there. This was a relief for Angelo, who for some months had seen it as a waste of his and everyone else's time.

Jankowski had other things to tend to, especially over the holidays, with drunks driving back from the casinos some fifty miles or more away, stopping occasionally to refuel both their trucks and themselves. Snowmobilers were also known to have a few too many and find trees in their way. All week long, the captain and his deputies were also on the lookout for what they called speeding *trolls*—tourists from the Lower Peninsula, *below the bridge*, who were under the impression there was nothing and nobody to look out for in the UP—except trees.

Angelo went home to Eagletown. He missed Lexi and was looking forward to spending Christmas together. Her raven hair, smooth and lustrous to her waist; her flashing black eyes; and her silky complexion—her beauty always surprised him after they had been apart. He was blown away all over again the moment he saw her. Blood rushed from his gut to his head and back down to his groin.

Between rounds of lovemaking, she related details of her days at Standing Rock. She fell into sadness all over again, until he comforted her, and they made love again. She wondered about Engadine. "Not much to tell," he said.

It was the first warm, sunny day in the spring of 2018, when they drove to their favorite quiet spot, North Bar Lake, near the town of Empire. They had the beach to themselves and took their first swim of the season in the warm, clear, shallow water before they ate their picnic lunch. They then strolled the short path across the low dune that separated North Bar from Lake Michigan, surrounded on both sides by dune grass and other native plants that helped hold the dune in place against the northwest winds. They hiked north along the shore of the big lake, to the huge bluffs of Sleeping Bear Dunes, especially aware, on this first day back, of its immensity and steepness. They had often climbed the giant dune from the lakeshore to the top, and then run back down. One day, they would try again, but not today.

When they turned back toward North Bar Lake, Angelo said, "Let's drive up to the top."

Lexi knew he would not be able to leave without taking in the views from the Sleeping Bear. They gathered their things and drove to Pierce Stocking Drive in the National Seashore. The drive wound through the trees, to the highest point, where they walked the path to the edge of the great sand cliff, 450 feet above the shoreline. She smiled at him out of the corner of her eyes.

"No, I can't see Wisconsin," he said, "but that doesn't mean I'm going to stop trying." He always found the very absurdity of seeing over the earth's curvature 100 miles to the other side to be more challenging than discouraging.

Lexi said, "I look for the point where the round sky meets the water."

"I love that too," he said.

Strolling over to the next viewing area, they looked north to the Manitou Islands—the two lost cubs of the Sleeping Bear legend.

Lexi said, "You want to be out there, don't you?"

"I need to go back sometime."

"I know. And you will."

With the elders' blessing he had chosen as a teen, to go to North Manitou Island for his vision quest. But, even after days of fasting, Angelo never felt the presence of Gitche Manitou, the Great Spirit. He had lit the ritual fires, laid out the tobacco, spoken to the great bald eagle and rocks and the trees and the bears and their cubs— but they did not speak back. He cried out to the spirits of the seven realms—but they did not cry back. He even prayed the way he had seen his Catholic grandmother pray in church. Nothing.

It was forbidden to tell anyone about what happened on your quest, but teenage boys, not infrequently, broke that rule among themselves. Although some of his friends blew off their own experiences, others, who came back proud of their newfound manhood, spoke with awe of actually seeing and even talking with the spirits.

Angelo returned home to his grandmother in the doublewide on Highway M-22, ashamed and defeated.

His father, who just happened to be there on one of his rare appearances, drunk as usual, ranted. "Didn't I tell you? It's all Indian mumbo-jumbo bullshit."

That day, for the first and only time, Angelo struck his father—hit him hard alongside his ear when he ducked. The force knocked the sloppy drunk to the floor. Angelo's grandmother, took the boy in her arms and never said a word. Moments passed before his father struggled to sit up, then flopped over on the floor again, and fell asleep.

When he finally awoke, he said, "Bullshit. It's all bullshit," and walked out the door. Once more, Angelo didn't know if he would ever see his father again.

Angelo hesitated for days before he finally made himself go to Me-me-was-be-min ("He who is observed"), the eldest of the elders, and confessed his failure. They took him to the healing lodge that night and tried every ritual they could. They had him on his knees, face-down near the sacred fire, tobacco, eagle feathers, and sacred medicines spread around him on the dirt floor. He could sense every elder of the tribe hovering over him. His eyes were closed but he could still see their dark shadows in his mind's eye. They spoke the words, they chanted the chants. Sometimes one or the other of them would stop and ask, "Do you feel it, do you feel the spirit?" and he would have to shake his head no. Then they would go back to their machinations until they would ask again, "Do you feel it?" Angelo was determined to have it be true. He tried with all his heart until two things slowly began to dawn on him: it wasn't going to happen and they weren't going to let him up until he told them what they wanted to hear. The next time they asked, "Do you feel the spirit?" Angelo looked up and smiled.

"Yes, I feel it," he said. He stood with a large grin on his face. He made the elders happy. They nodded and smiled to each other and shook each other's hands as well as his.

Lexi was the only person to whom Angelo had ever told the whole story. They both knew he would have to go back some day. But, now, on this sunny spring day, they left the dunes area and drove back to Eagletown.

CHAPTER 4

The Proposal

The next day, Angelo met with the Tribal Council. They voted to join other tribes and their supporters to move their Water Protector efforts on to Flint.

Angelo and Lexi loaded his pickup with bottled water and covered it with an old tarp. They were mostly silent during the first couple hours of the drive, until they stopped for lunch in West Branch. At the restaurant, Angelo stared at the menu, not speaking.

"I'm sorry for your sadness," Lexi said. "What's going on?"

"I wish you couldn't always see through me," he said. "It's nothing. I'm just not feeling good about things right now. I was supposed to be a big hockey star—but look what I did with that. I was stuck in Engadine while the big stuff was going on at Standing Rock and Mackinac. I come home and get nothing but odd jobs here and there, until this Flint thing comes along. I'm supposed to be a man, Lex. You have a good job at the co-op and I'm going nowhere."

"I hated you in high school when you were a big hockey star."

"So you have often told me."

She smiled at him and said, "Yes."

"Yes what?" Angelo asked. He saw the look of intrigue on her face. "What's going on in that brain of yours?"

"Yes, I will marry you," she said, laughing. "You have been wanting to ask me but are afraid."

"Alexi Pullman," said Angelo, "you are truly loco. We talked about this a long time ago. You said you didn't want to get married. You said we were as married as we were ever going to be."

"Ever and never are both a long time. We are not who we were ever ago. It's time."

"I'm not proud of where I am right now."

"You are a good man. You have a good heart. I love you and I trust you. Your time is coming. I am not afraid for you. You should not be either."

"I didn't think it was fair of me to ask you."

The timing of the waitress's appearance at their table was not ideal. "Can I bring you two something to drink? Are you ready to order?"

Lexi grinned at her and said, "We're getting married."

Angelo smiled down at his menu.

"Oh, my gosh," the waitress said. "I figured you two were already married. Well, congratulations! That's great news ... I hope."

Angelo said. "Have a large. Whatever you want." When the food arrived, he tried to act happy.

Back in the car, on the way to Flint, Angelo was quiet again for a long while, and then broke out in laughter.

Lexi waited a mile for an explanation. He said he was

just thinking about things back on the reservation. Empty fields stretched out to the east and west from the freeway.

"And?" she said.

"What was the 'rezziest' thing you ever did or heard about?"

"'Rezziest'?"

"Like knocking my drunken father to the floor when I was a kid."

"That made you laugh?"

"Talking about getting married got me thinking about stuff like that. First, sad stuff: my drunken father, or your brother getting stabbed by his white fiancée, or me quitting college over a hassle with my coach. How stupid rezzy it all was. Then I just started thinking about sillier things. My dad had this car once. You had to climb over the front seat into the backseat to get out."

"Speaking of my brother, I've got a story for you. Mark and his buddy Lenny got jobs downstate, in Detroit. So, they take off in an old rez beater that gets like twelve miles to a gallon and they only have enough money for gas to get down there. On the way down, Mark lights up a cigarette with their very last match. So, no more matches and no lighter. They can't stop for fear of using up too much gas. So, guess what? They chain smoked the entire four and a half hours to Detroit."

"That's Mark, all right."

"Oh, but I forgot the part about the pee bottles."

Angelo laughed and said, "We had a blanket on our back door for a curtain because our blind broke."

"Every true rez house has a blanket as a curtain," Lexi said. "So, when I was little, we were at a powwow in Grand Rapids. I watched two young guys walk up to a port-a-potty and rock it back and forth and then run away. A guy comes out and slugs a woman in the face just because she was the first person he saw."

"My dad always wanted a convertible. He takes a saw-zall to his Ford subcompact and makes his own."

Lexi said, "It would all be funny if it wasn't so sad."

Angelo thought for a minute, then said, "I might have been one of those kids you saw rocking the port-a-potty."

They rode along in silence for a few miles. Lexi tapped him on the leg. "Are we avoiding the elephant in the car? You haven't answered me. I proposed to you and you haven't answered me."

"Just having fun."

"Bullshit."

"Lex, let's face it. I have wanted us to get married for a long time now. Nothing would make me happier. I just don't believe I deserve it right now. I don't want us to start on the wrong foot, and I'm afraid that I'm definitely on the wrong foot right now. I appreciate and love the faith you have in me; I just don't have it in myself. I feel a little like I did when I couldn't find the spirits on North Manitou—and I don't want to fake it with you the way I did then."

"I understand," Lexi said. "I don't want you to feel you have to fake it. I can wait."

"There's another thing. I'm not just feeling down. I'm feeling angry. I want to hurt someone or a lot of some-ones. Remember I told you I quit hockey at Lake Superior because the coach tried to turn me into a goon? What I didn't tell you—what I didn't want to tell you—what I didn't want to admit to myself—there was a part of me that liked it. I actually wanted to bust heads. There's a part of me that's always wanted that. A part of me that's done that, even. Ever since hockey in Traverse City, I have never felt whole. The white players at any level never really accepted me. The guys on the rez thought I was trying to be a bigshot. Even my best friend."

"My brother."

"Yeah, even Mark."

"I even felt that way before you left for college," Lexi said.

"I know. But I *was* good, Lex, and I loved it at the same time I hated it. It always made me mad. I always wanted to hit somebody. I hated that coach, but I also hated myself because I enjoyed being the goon. That's not who I want to be, Lex. That's not who you should marry."

"But I've seen the kind, strong, spiritual man I love. The compassionate young man who came home from college when Mark was murdered, which was the first time I ever liked you at all. That's when I first thought maybe I could fall in love with you. Now you are the man who looks out over Lake Michigan to see Wisconsin, the one who knows better but still tries. The one who didn't see the spirits when he was fourteen, the one who even now has doubts, but the one who is still on a quest. You may never find all you are looking for, Ang, but you will also never stop trying. You may feel some anger but you are so full of love."

"I'm afraid, Lex. You are the only person I could admit that to. I'm scared. People talk about experience adding another layer to the onion. I have had plenty of experiences, but when I peel away the layers, the onion is hollow in the center. I'm afraid that's me. I can't marry you if I'm hollow. I want to—but I can't."

"I know you have a solid core, Ang, but you have to know it for yourself. And, you will. But listen, this is the last time I am proposing to you. When and if you ever think you're ready, you're going to have to do the asking."

"I'll grant you that. Only fair. One day, I will."

"Maybe I'll say yes. If you play your cards right, that is."

The old farmers market in Flint was a drop-off site for bottled water. When they pulled into the parking lot, Lexi pointed and smiled. "Look at their shiny trucks and trailers. We have all those old rezzy tarps and towels and blankets in back of this old rezzy truck. We better get busy before people notice."

Angelo really did love her. How could he not? Someday, he thought. Someday.

CHAPTER 5

Flint

School was out for the day, and Angelo could see that the kids and their families couldn't wait to see the Pistons' Lamarcus Townsend and the Red Wings' Perry Karas. The fans that could afford it wore their favorite players jerseys—more Pistons than Wings, but there were even a few Karas hockey sweaters scattered among them. Angelo guessed that the planned appearance by Charlie Birnbaum, Flint's representative in the US Congress, was almost an afterthought.

Lamarcus and Perry, with their agent and some of the Pistons' and Red Wings' management, came from Detroit with vans full of bottled water. They joined Flint civic and neighborhood leaders, a large Native American contingent, and National Guardsmen to form conveyor lines to haul the cases of water away.

Angelo and Lexi added their Eagletown palettes to the collection and then got in the line. The work went so well that people were actually laughing and having fun—all kinds of people, Angelo thought—complete strangers—working together. *Why couldn't things always work this way?*

Lamarcus and Perry held mini-clinics on the old school playground next door. Ballers gathered around the playground's hoops while the smaller hockey group took to the makeshift rink on another stretch of concrete for some drills. Angelo had always followed the Wings closely, and Perry Karas especially caught his eye as he worked with the kids. Karas was the latest young "feenom," the next Gordie Howe or Stevie Yzerman. Angelo swallowed his resentment and offered to help, if only to prove that he had some stick himself.

Perry could not have been more gracious. He introduced himself as they shook hands. Angelo said, "I know who you are. You play the game well. I'm Angelo RoundSky."

Perry hesitated a moment. "Somehow that name rings a bell. Thanks for watching the Wings."

While Angelo helped Perry and the Wings with the hockey drills, Lexi edged her way over to the crowd watching Lamarcus Townsend work with the boys and girls on the basketball court.

When the drills were winding down, Angelo saw Lexi heading his way, holding the hand of a little girl. With them was a woman he guessed to be the girl's mother. Lexi introduced Tina and her mother. "Tell him what you told me, Ruby."

Mrs. Ortega shook Angelo's hand and said, apologetically, "I don't want to impose with all our troubles." She did go on, though, and gave him a short summary of what she and Lexi had been talking about: Tina sick from lead poisoning and her boy, Henry, in the hospital even sicker.

"I thought I heard the water's better now?" Angelo said.

"They say it's better with a filter but I'm not so sure. Why else is Henry still sick? I know the state stopped delivery of bottled water—but look around. People don't trust it, so all of you good people keep bringing us bottled water, thank goodness."

There was more. She had lost her job when the water went bad. She had a college degree from across the street at U of M Flint; once worked as a supervisor at the Van Slyke Road Chevy plant. But that job went away even before the water went bad. "Automation, mostly," she said. "About eighty thousand people worked for GM back in the day; and now it's down to about seven thousand. I'm one of those lost their job." She waited tables in a restaurant until they had to close because of no water.

"Things are bad here," she said. "Been bad for a long, long time, even before the water went bad. Population half of what it once was. I don't see anything getting any better for a long time. I'd get out if I could, but where we going to go?"

"And your husband? Is he working?"

"No husband, honey. We're divorced and he's in jail."

Angelo patted her on the shoulder. "All I can say is I'm sorry."

Mrs. Ortega nodded and said, "Well, excuse my bad manners. I should just thank you all for coming."

"Where is your son? What hospital?" asked Lexi.

"Hurley Hospital. Pediatric Center."

"Would they let us visit him sometime?" Lexi asked.

"Oh, don't feel like you have to do that."

"We'd be honored to," said Angelo.

Her face brightened. "I'm sure he'd be happy for the company. Lamarcus Townsend has almost adopted him.

He and Perry have been so good to all the kids there. They bring them hats and jerseys and all. Lamarcus even brought Henry a pair of brand-new Pistons basketball shoes."

"We can't match that," Angelo said.

"I didn't mean …"

Lexi smiled and said, "We'd just like to do our part."

"He'd love a visit," said Perry Karas, surprising them from behind. "And so would the other kids there."

Angelo backed away a step while Mrs. Ortega gave Perry a big smile and a hug. "These are my new friends, Perry," Mrs. Ortega said, as Perry squatted down to hug Tina.

"I'm Lexi," she said and shook Perry's hand. "I'm with him."

"He did a great job today, helping me with the hockey kids," said Perry.

"We promise we'll try to stop by the hospital. And we'll be saying some prayers," said Lexi.

When Tina and her mother walked off with Perry to visit with Lamarcus Townsend, Lexi held Angelo, her head in his chest. When she finally looked up, he saw tears in her eyes.

"Lex, I know how bad you feel about all this, but you can't take it so personally. It just brings you down. All we can do is what we can do. And we will."

"I can't help it. You know that."

A few minutes later, a murmur passed through the crowd. They spotted a white-haired man shaking hands as he made his way toward a makeshift stage in one of the market shelters. It was a sunny day, enhanced by his sunny smile, and reflected in the expressions of the people who spontaneously created a path for him.

"Charlie Birnbaum," Angelo told Lexi. "The congressman from around here. Rumor is he may run for governor."

"I just hope he can help these people," Lexi said.

"He seems to be a pretty straight shooter."

"A sincere white politician. Where have I heard that before?"

"Right. We'll see."

"Thank you, thank you all for coming," Birnbaum began. "It's wonderful that you can enjoy a day like this with so much suffering in this city. Through no fault of your own, you have been made the victims of big bureaucracies gone bad—as big bureaucracies often do—and thoughtless, callous leaders on top of it all. But, at least for today, for this little break, I hope you are having a good time.

"We all need to thank Perry Karas from the Red Wings, and, most of all, Lamarcus Townsend from the Pistons, for making all this happen. I had a chance to talk with Perry, who as you all know, is having a terrible time from the concussion he took but promised me he'll be back on the ice as soon as he is able."

The crowd cheered.

"He also promises he will be back here with the Wings on a regular basis. He told me how moved the team has been by your situation and they want to thank you for letting them into your lives. They won't forget you. He also tells me that Lamarcus is the real heart behind all this. Lamarcus, come on up here."

Lamarcus Townsend and Charlie Birnbaum shook hands. The ex-Piston rebounder towered over Charlie as the congressman tried to hold their hands up high together, with only marginal success.

Lamarcus spoke. "I never had much to say when they interviewed me after a game. People thought that I was too ignorant to speak or too ungrateful for the opportunity I had to play basketball on such great teams and to make a lot of money doing it. I may not be the brightest but I am smart enough to see how fucked up things were here in Flint. Oooops, sorry kids. I shouldn't have said that. Maybe they were right about why I didn't talk so much. But, seriously, let me tell you something. I was always grateful. The real reason I didn't like to talk was I was still so focused on the game, win or lose. Now, I'm just as focused on you, and we ain't gonna lose. I am with you, and I ain't goin' nowhere until this problem is solved.

"Mr. Birnbaum, sir, I know you come back some to help these folks. I just hope you can do even more when they elect you governor. I wish I could vote for you."

Birnbaum stepped up again and took the handheld mic. "Governor, eh? We'll have to see about that. Maybe that's some of that fake news. But I *do* have some *good* news to share with you today, and I'd like your mayor to tell you about it. Here she is, Ms. Juliet Mason."

Angelo nudged Lexi. "Talk is cheap." He looked around at faces and saw both hope and despair. He and Lexi could identify with those feelings.

The mayor was all smiles as she stepped onto the platform and shook the congressman's hand. She thanked Birnbaum and seemed very happy to be standing close to Lamarcus. Angelo struggled to pay attention until he heard her say, "I am delighted to announce that the U.S. Congress just passed a bill that will bring over $120 million to help fix some of our water problems, including replacing the old lead pipes." She raised her fist in the air to much applause, and then spoke again. "But that's not enough. I know that—and you know that, Congressman. We all know that. We have so many people in and around our city who are working so hard and giving so much, but we need so much more. Our state officials just told us that everything is A-OK now, our water is fit to drink. They have stopped state support for bottled water as of now, as you well know. But these are the same people who for years told us we didn't have a problem in the first place.

"I don't trust them, and most people in this city don't trust them. We know for a fact that at least a hundred thousand of our citizens do not have clean drinking water. Congressman Birnbaum, you have to keep fighting for us, sir—and I know you will."

Birnbaum began to wrap things up. "I don't know who Lamarcus has been talking to but I don't know if I will be running for governor, or anything else. What I *do* know is it won't matter who we elect if we don't change our system in a fundamental way. You can throw out the rascals and bring in a whole raft of new people. But, you know what? Our system of government, both here and nationally, is so broken that those new people—even good people with the best intentions in the world—will too soon get caught up in the same old way of doing business along party lines; raising money for the next election and letting big money and special interests show them the way. Just imagine if we put Lamarcus on the Red Wings or Perry on the Pistons. As good as they are as athletes, they wouldn't be much good for their new teams. All their marvelous talent would be wasted. So, here's my message: *It's not enough to change the players; we have to change the game.*"

CHAPTER 6

Steve's Bistro

Alone in the private dining room at Steve's Bistro, a classy, well-appointed place in Fenton, only a few miles from Flint, Charlie Birnbaum sipped his martini and thought back to the gathering that afternoon. He could have done a better job with his short speech, he mused. Maybe he shouldn't have said anything political at all. People were there for the athletes, not him.

He looked forward to seeing Lana Hartman again. It had been a while. She'd taken his call and agreed to meet with him. That was a start. The first time he saw her in action, she was a young staffer for then Michigan Senator Ron Goodwin. Charlie remembered, with a smile, that at the last minute she had been stuck dealing with a delegation of auto execs. She could think on her feet.

He was halfway through his drink when the door opened. Unlike his normal rumpled appearance, Lana was always put together. She wore a navy sheath dress, a shawl, and pumps. Steve Finestra, owner of the bistro, accompanied her to the table, where Birnbaum rose to give her a hug. He said, "You won't believe what I was just thinking about."

Steve pulled out her chair. She pointed to the congress-man's drink. "Martini?"

"Of course."

She asked Steve for the same.

"I'll leave you to deal with this old crank," Steve said as he left.

"I see he knows you well," said Lana.

"The auto guys were headed your way. They were pissed about something," Charlie said.

"Don't remind me. I knew nothing about the car business."

"But, by the time I got there, you had them eating out of your hand."

"So you say—but all I did was listen," she said.

"That was always your best trick. A rare commodity in D.C.," said Charlie.

"At that moment, I didn't have much choice. And, Congressman, as I recall, when you finally got there, you didn't offer me very much help."

"Like I said, you were in complete control, and I enjoyed sitting back and watching you perform your magic."

"It did turn out well, didn't it?" She paused to watch the TV at the end of the room. A local reporter was com-menting on the congressional money dump for Flint. "But you didn't get me here to talk old times."

"Tell me, how is it going in academia these days? Do you like being a law professor?"

"Actually, Charlie, I'm loving it. You remember Joss, Jocelyn Urabuna? She and I got married a year ago, when she left her job at Yale and started up her own firm in Ann Arbor. I love teaching at the law school, and she's doing well with her firm. We live in a beautiful, old Victorian barn of a house on the Huron River. All's right with the world. I barely miss the Washington rough and tumble."

"But, you *do* miss it?"

She leaned forward, tilted her head, and smiled. "You're getting serious about this governor thing."

"I've had quite a day." After discussing Flint, the money from Congress, the generosity of Lamarcus Townsend and Perry Karas, Charlie continued. "Lamarcus tried to get me to stay for dinner with some of the locals."

"You probably should have. I'm not sure what we're here for, but it probably could have waited another day."

"Are you kidding me? I wouldn't eat there. That water is poisoned, haven't you heard?"

"Charlie, you're awful," Lana laughed.

"I may be awful but I ain't stupid. I'm not about to drink that shit."

"I'm sure they would find you some bottled water, Congressman."

"I'm not so sure. Lamarcus was committed to getting me into the down and dirty. I think he would have made me drink the real thing." He shifted to the subject of the bottled water that was being delivered to Flint. "But, as needed as it is right now, those bottling companies are ripping off our state, draining our aquifers for almost nothing, and making millions on it. We're trying to solve one water problem with another. Makes me frustrated and angry. On the other hand, I have to tell you, I was really humbled and awed at how those poor people are coping."

"Did you confirm the rumors for them, Charlie?"

"I was tempted but I didn't think it was the time or place. Today was about the kids and their sports heroes. Besides, I haven't made up my mind yet. That's why we're here. You're going to help me with that decision. But first, just let me mention, the veal saltimbocca here is to die for. Just so you know."

After they ordered from a young waiter, Charlie asked Lana for her views on Michigan's state constitution. Water was the problem, he explained, but the constitution was the critical subject.

Lana said, "I've been doing some homework—you have my attention and maybe my interest. But, I need to know why you think we need a new constitution."

"I'm not going for a whole new constitution. I wish I could, but that is ruled out for now. But we don't need just a new deal, we need a new deck." He finished his second martini. "Not a new team, but a new game."

The news station on the TV, appropriately enough, had moved on from the weather to sports.

"A new game," Lana repeated. "Nice campaign slogan. May even get you elected. But, what does it mean?"

"It's way more than a slogan, Lana. It sums up what I truly believe—and have for some time, since way back in D.C., before all this mess we're in now. The constitution may have been all well and good for its time but it no longer fits the times we live in. As the Peer Progressives say, our operating system was designed before there were railroads."

"Wait a minute, Charlie. Are you talking about the state or the US constitution?"

He laughed. "I'm not sure there's enough security around here for us to have the latter conversation, so let's just start here in Michigan, okay?"

"That's a relief. So, seriously, if we can't have a constitutional Convention, what do you have in mind?"

"What do *I* want in a new constitution or, in this case, in a constitutional amendment? I'm not really sure. But I believe the three things we all need in our lives are dignity, meaning, and community. I want an amendment that will create a framework for more people to obtain more of those three things in their lives.

"The US constitution was grounded in a theory of government for a revolutionary time. We now find ourselves in another revolutionary time. We see it as voter revolt, both from the right and the left; both in our state and nationally. That's what got your friend, the Boy King, elected. That's what the pots and pans were telling us here in Michigan. That's what we're going to see here again next November."

Lana shook her head. Her eyes widened. "If you're comparing the people who put that asshole in the White House to the founders of our country, I'm not the woman for this job."

"They had scumbags in their ranks too, don't forget. But, Lana, people know the system is broken. It's just not working for them." He held up his water glass again, as self-evident proof. "That's their message. They elected a President they saw as a strong leader—never mind that he's a narcissistic demagogue. They wanted a new sheriff to ride in and clean up the town. Unfortunately, that's not what they got."

"How will an amendment to the Michigan constitution help?"

"We don't need heroes. We need a new game. All of Michigan's constitutions—there have been a few—started from the big one. As they should, of course. I'm not interested in being a separatist. But we need an amendment or two that will change our basic structure, that will make us a true government that is of, for, and by the people. A government that gives people a picture of a new future they can trust in; not a promise of returning to the fifties."

"Okay. Who do we get to be *our* Founding Fathers and mothers? Or is it 'founding parents'? A blue-ribbon drafting committee?"

"God, no! Dammit. No blue-ribbon committee. I'm beginning to think you haven't been listening to me," he said with a typical chortle.

She smiled. She had a hunch that would get him going. "Sorry, my friend, but I'm listening now. No blue-ribbon committees. Got it. But listen, like I said, I've been doing some homework myself."

A different server appeared with a young man at her side to remove their plates. Lana had forgotten they had even been served. She looked at her barely touched food.

"Now, how about some dessert?" Charlie asked.

He's good, she smiled to herself. The old bastard is as good as ever. I almost forgot to eat. Aloud she said, "Oh, god, no! Charlie, you've tempted me enough for one night. Look, I have some ideas of my own that I've been learning about in my research. I think they are in line with what you are after."

"Great, that's why I asked you to do this. I know you."

"You think? Even my conservative Republican grandfather isn't so sure he knows me anymore."

"Even he will be proud of you all over again when you get this thing done."

"*If,* Charlie, *if.* I'm interested ... I'm, let's say ...

intrigued, but I haven't committed to anything yet. And neither have you, for god's sake."

"*Yet*," smiled Charlie. "I think I like the sound of that."

The next few minutes, she talked about efforts at major changes in Iceland, British Columbia, and Ontario. Lana explained that they had a lot of involvement from regular rank-and-file people rather than officials, basically picking people by lot to design new electoral systems.

"By lot?"

"Yes, almost like standard jury selection."

"Now, you're talking."

"In Iceland, they actually created what some called a 'crowd-sourced constitution.'"

"Love it."

"What I need to tell you, though, is that in all these instances, even though they went at it with a great deal of thought and enthusiasm, and people voted overwhelmingly in favor in a public referendum, the bottom line in all cases was that the proposals were defeated at the hands of the old parliamentary parties, and it was back to business as usual."

"Oh, bullshit. Been there," Charlie said.

"We've both been there. So, the bottom line is that it all came to naught. So far, at least. In all three cases—British Columbia, Ontario, and most of all, Iceland—a process loaded with enthusiasm and general acceptance from the public was blown out of the water. Bupkis, as you say."

"I hate a sad ending, Lana. But the truth is, I'm actually encouraged and excited."

"I think I'm there too, Charlie, but there are some big red flags."

"Maybe just yellow ones. We have to be smarter. We

have to be—shall I say it—much better politicians? And, baby, you and I are the ones who can do that."

"Oh, god, I hope so. Otherwise we're fucked. We could easily be fucked before they even drop the puck."

"You girls and your sports analogies!" laughed Charlie. "But, you're right."

"A lot of people, not just politicos, are going to think we're crazy from day one. They'll make fun of us, if nothing else. And, don't think for a minute that D.C. isn't going to go ballistic, both Congress and Boykin. Maybe even the Supreme Court."

"Boykin is going to be Boykin. We'll have to find a balance and stick to and protect this state's business without making people think we're separatists."

"That's a fine line, Congressman. A tricky line. We need an optimally permeable membrane if we're going to stay alive."

"'Optimally permeable.' I love it. I think, Professor Hartman, you mean we need to keep open, two-way lines of feedback while at the same time keeping our asses covered. I'm glad you're taking it on, Lana. I was pretty sure you would, but I won't say I wasn't worried."

"I haven't said I would yet, have I?"

"Of course, you have."

"You're slippery as ever, my friend. If you're in, I'm afraid I am too. You got me—or maybe you'll just be stuck with me."

On the short drive back to Flint, Charlie Birnbaum smiled as he reminded himself of the way he and Lana had been able to work across the aisle on past projects. She was a born-and-bred Republican but she knew how to get things done. They would have to be better than ever this time.

PART TWO

CHAPTER 7

Michigan Speaks

In early January 2019, Angelo and Lexi both received official letters from the new Governor, Charles Birnbaum, inviting them to attend a conference called "Michigan Speaks." All adult Michigan residents were invited to participate in the conference that would be held in Detroit's Cobo Hall. The governor's goal was to get input from a broad cross-section of the state's residents. Ads with similar invitations appeared on television and radio, and in newspapers throughout the state. If they were interested in attending, people were asked to respond by postage-paid return mail, email, on the Michigan Speaks website, or its Facebook page. Special invitations were extended to key members of the state Legislature, mayors, union officials, and key company management. There was going to be a new amendment to the state constitution regarding the electoral process.

Lexi immediately wanted to sign up, but Angelo, still skeptical of "the man" and unsure of his talent for such things, had to be persuaded. He agreed only if she was going to be with him. He wasn't too concerned. Each person who RSVPed with a yes, would be issued a number. Five thousand of those numbers would be drawn at random. Those individuals would actually take part in the conference. Their chances were slim to none, he thought.

The drawing would be televised live on local newscasts all over the state. The slick ads made it look like the typical lottery-drawing event. The first ten numbers would be drawn on the air, both to promote the event and to illustrate the transparency and random fairness of the process. The rest would be revealed via email to those who had confirmed their interest in attending.

Local news ratings were much higher than normal that evening. Not only people whose numbers were among the eligible watched, but many more tuned in just out of curiosity. Lexi and Angelo sat together on the couch in their two-bedroom home at the end of a cul de sac. "Oh, well," Lexi said, when neither of their numbers were called during the broadcast. Angelo relaxed.

That changed later when, just before midnight that night, they spotted number 789 on the email list. She grabbed his arm and shrieked, "You made it!"

"I don't believe it," he said.

Angelo RoundSky, lottery number 789, had played junior hockey in Detroit's Joe Louis Arena—The Joe—but he had never been inside Cobo Hall. He was not sure he wanted to be there on this cold February day either. He felt less confident than when he played in the championships next door. But Lexi had insisted he attend.

Before he left her at the hotel in Birch Run for his drive downtown, she kept telling him his time was coming, this might be the time. He was doing it for her sake, for their sake. He knew he needed to think of all the hardships of their people, and the courage and determination of all the Water Protectors and the people of Flint. He was also doing it, she had said, for Henry Ortega, the boy they had visited in the hospital last year.

At a long table in Cobo's entrance hall, Angelo gave his numbered invitation to one of several receptionists. She handed him a blue-and-green folder. Inside the giant conference room, he felt his stomach tighten. Tables as far as he could see, hundreds of round tables, each with a desktop computer and eleven chairs. Several viewing screens hung around the cavernous rectangular room. Hovering over a big stage with a podium was a much larger screen. The room was thronged with people, some seated at the tables, chatting with one or two tablemates, but most people were milling around, chatting in small groups. Angelo headed for the end of the room with the coffee urns, drew himself a cup of black coffee and began looking for his table number.

Five thousand people, he thought. Five thousand people to discuss one or more amendments. How the hell is that supposed to work? He knew what he would do: play the role of the silent, stoic Indian .

Two men were already seated at table 53. He set down his coffee and nodded when the two smiled his way. He didn't sit. He turned his gaze to the vast room again and tried once more to absorb it all, even the girders and heating ducts, the deafening noise but, most of all, the people. The two men at his table were friends from the same town, the nearby Detroit suburb of Roseville. Both expressed surprise their numbers had been chosen.

"What were the chances?" one said.

They had never heard of Eagletown. Angelo didn't want to go into it. "Up north, near Traverse City," he said.

"You've come a long way to get here then."

"We're staying in Flint. I just drove in from Flint this morning," Angelo said as he took a sip of burned coffee.

"They have it tough in Flint," one said.

"Bad there," the other added. They smiled and turned back to their conversation.

Angelo opened the folder to find the day's agenda and a copy of the current state constitution.

At the appointed time, a well-dressed woman walked up to the podium and asked people to take their seats. "Good morning and welcome to Cobo Hall. My name is Lana Hartman," she said. "Governor Birnbaum has appointed me as steward for this constitution project. We have invited five thousand Michigan citizens to join together in what we have called "Michigan Speaks"—and that is exactly what we want you to do today. I'm glad to say that almost everyone we invited made it."

While she talked procedural and housekeeping details, Angelo racked his brain trying to place her. She was about his age, a hockey player, he was pretty sure. Goalie for the Draytonware girls?

She continued. "A presidential candidate way back in 1928, Al Smith, once famously said: 'The cure for the evils of democracy is more democracy.' That exactly sums up our purpose here. Today is one step in that democratic process toward a more democratic end goal. You are the lucky winners of that lottery. Michigan is lucky you are here. Right now, I am lucky and proud to introduce the man who made all this happen. He loves this state. He loves democracy. He is my friend and longtime colleague, Governor Charlie Birnbaum."

Angelo was impressed when the Governor, despite his sixty plus years, loped onto the stage with the energy and grace of a much younger man. During his campaign, Birnbaum had reminded voters he was once a state champion hurdler. He could still get over the obstacles in his way.

He and Lana Hartman hugged and he looked out from the podium with the same childlike joy that was now associated with him. He thanked Lana and engaged the audience in some call and response. Are you proud to be a Michigander? YES. Are our best days ahead of us? YES. Are we up to facing the human suffering in Flint? YES. It went on like this for a while. He was good at it.

Next, he stressed his recurring themes about how impersonal hierarchies, both public and private, control our lives and how the system itself is broken. He repeated and elaborated on his tagline "It's not the players; it's the game."

"Unlike our President," he said, "I make no claim to being a hero riding in on a white horse, armed with a silver bullet, to save you. I'm just a Charlie, not a Boy King. I am a we-the-people guy. I know we need 'the people' to fix things. We can't just mouth the words; we need to walk the talk. That's where today comes in. We want to hear what your *concerns* are, what your *dreams* are. And, it's perfectly okay if you dream big.

"Some people say we should move slowly—make incremental improvements. And well we should. There are improvements we can get started on right away. But sometimes small changes are only worth just that-small change. We need BIG CHANGE. So, dream big. Be bold. Be audacious. And we will see what happens. I'm still a hurdler, you know. Between us, we'll jump each hurdle as it comes. So, let's go for it!"

Governor Birnbaum stepped aside to let Lana return to the mic. As this happened, a map of Michigan's two peninsulas, with stars marking where the five thousand attendees came from appeared on all the TV screens. A loud burst of applause erupted in the room.

"How exciting is *that*?!" Lana asked, to more applause. "That looks a lot like Michigan, doesn't it? So, let's get on with hearing *you* speak. What are the issues, values, and structures you believe need to be addressed? We will do that in steps, asking you to discuss and then list your responses to questions or statements, responses we will then post in aggregate on the screens."

She explained that each table had ten participants and one trained facilitator. Each group was to identity a volunteer participant to record on the computer any conclusions reached by the group. This information would then be fed to a tech group that would summarize the findings on the screens.

"You have a wonderful opportunity in front of you," Lana said, "but a very difficult challenge. Think of what you are about to do as putting together a giant jigsaw puzzle and each of you is one piece of the puzzle. You are not here to represent any group or constituency back home. You are not here as an expert. You are just *you*, an important piece of the puzzle. And we have all the pieces we need to complete that puzzle by the end of the day."

At Angelo's table, when, as part of an environmental scan, they listed what was going on in the world outside of Michigan, a Ford-plant machine operator expressed some frustration. "I thought this meeting was called *Michigan* Speaks. I thought we were supposed to be talking about our own problems in *this* state, not trying to fix the problems of the world."

A grade-school teacher from Pinkney responded, "That's exactly one of the problems in this state. We don't pay enough attention to what's going on in the world. We seem to think it doesn't affect us—but I would say that almost every problem we have is somehow tied in with something going on outside of us, things going on in every place, from China to the Middle East to, of course, Washington D.C. We are not immune to these outside issues and we can't bury our heads in the sand about them." She got nods of approval from around the table. The man from Ford sat back, perhaps unconvinced but ready to move on.

Angelo was happy to remain quiet and let others have their say. He couldn't help himself, though, when they talked about the environment, especially water. He discussed the Water Protectors at Standing Rock. "National troubles," he said, "eventually become local trouble." As the process funneled down into Michigan issues, there was the threat of a spill from the Enbridge Line 5 into the Great Lakes. "Does anyone remember the Kalamazoo River Enbridge oil spill just back in 2010?" he asked. "One of the biggest inland spills in US history."

He explained that water was Michigan's greatest resource, and Nestlé was taking millions of gallons out of the ground for bottled water. They pay the state $200 for a permit, then make millions. "It's like they're printing money," he said.

He saved Flint for last. "If it wasn't for what's going on in Flint," he said, "we probably wouldn't even be here today."

Later that day, on the summary screen, at the top of the list was lack of trust in the state Government and no sense of how that trust could be regained. Michigan once took pride in its public schools. Now they were ranked toward the bottom of the nation. Next was public health, with Flint the prime example; and the future of the Great Lakes and other important Michigan waterways. The economy was also on the list.

Goals and objectives scrolled across the screen: Transparency in government leading to trust. Renewed emphasis on and pride in public education, K-12 and beyond, including community colleges and other technical/vocational training programs. Greater protection of our environment, with emphasis on our water resources. Dedication to public health; especially for our children, the poor, and the elderly. A greater safety net of services for low-income citizens. Foster economic growth for the 21st century. Invest in our cities. We can't have a great state if we don't have great cities.

The next phase, Lana said, would be for a group to take the ideas generated today and draft an amendment or two. She would say more about that at the reception in the next room.

Angelo stood up and shook hands with his tablemates, feeling slightly more enthusiastic and friendly. Still, he kept a wait-and-see attitude. *Draft what? Could they really do something, make a difference?* He had lived his life skeptical of white people's promises. For now, he allowed himself to carry some hope into the reception.

CHAPTER 8

The Drawing

Angelo's curiosity was aroused as he waited at one of the several open bars scattered about the room. People had formed dozens of small groups, drinking, talking, laughing. *So, this is how politics is done*, he thought. There was another platform stage set against a wall, with a podium and something that looked like a huge ten-gallon hat on the floor. *What's that about?*

He felt a hand on his shoulder. Lana Hartman had a big smile on her face. "Angelo RoundSky," she said. "I spotted your name on the list. Man, it's been years." She reached out to shake his hand.

His face brightened in surprise. "I told myself when you walked onto the stage, I know that lady. She's that goalie I used to watch; that girl who played better than the boys."

"You were pretty damn good yourself. You scored goals for the boys' teams and I stopped them for the girls' teams. Such fun."

"You did a good job here, today."

"You guys, all five thousand of you, did all the work. So, what have you been up to since our hockey days?"

Angelo gave a rueful chuckle. "Part of a year at Lake Superior state is all. The coach and I didn't see things the same way."

"I get that. And, now?"

"I guess you could say I'm an environmentalist." He described the work of the Water Protectors and Line 5, stuff he was sure she already knew about. And Flint. He said he was pissed.

She nodded. "A tragic situation. There's another hockey guy who's been working in Flint.

"Perry Karas. We met there. Just quick."

"His number got drawn to be here. He's been part of this all day."

Angelo mentioned the concussion.

"Unlucky for him, lucky for us. Never too many hockey players. He's going to have a part in the drawing this evening."

"Drawing?"

"Twenty-five of you will be asked to help draft the amendment. I hope your name is drawn, Angelo. We could use a Water Protector in the group."

"And another hockey player? We're all troublemakers, you know. Especially me."

"Angelo, you know how to score."

When it was his turn at the bar, he decided he would just order a Coke. He wasn't sure he could handle anything stronger right now. Did he want his name drawn or not? Or did he want to just go back home. He wouldn't mind being home, hanging out with Lexi, doing odd jobs and relaxing. If his name was drawn, as usual, he would be the only Native among white people. It never felt good. He took his Coke and walked toward one of the hors d'oeuvres tables, not sure he could even eat anything.

He joined and quickly left a few conversations. Not everyone had a positive experience like he had. One person complained of a table member dominating their discussions, another complained about a guy who considered himself a law expert and put down everyone else's input, and another complained about a woman who took a cynical stance on everything throughout the whole day.

Near the stage, one of the two men from Roseville he had met first thing in the morning stopped him. "You know Lana Hartman?"

"A little bit. We played high-school hockey at the same time, years ago."

The man gestured toward the platform. "What's with that hat? What's that all about?"

Just then Lana appeared on the stage and stood at the podium, with the crowd moving in her direction. She explained the process. There would be a blind drawing. Those selected would help draft the amendment. "Or amendments," she said. "We should get a dynamic mix of people. Whatever happens, whoever we get from this terrific group will do just great."

Next, she asked Lamarcus Townsend and Perry Karas to the stage. They waved and bumped fists with fans as they moved through the enthusiastic crowd. After waiting for the applause to die down, Lana spoke again. "These two guys brought with them one of their closest friends, a young man from Flint who they have virtually adopted."

Ruby Ortega came in from the hallway, pushing her teenage son in his wheelchair, accompanied by his sister,

Tina, and an African American woman who, Angelo thought, could have been Halle Berry's younger sister.

Lana announced, "Please welcome Henry Ortega, his mother Ruby, his sister Tina, and his doctor Dr. Julia Majors from Flint's Hurley Hospital Pediatric Center."

Townsend and Karas lifted the wheelchair with Henry onto the stage; while Ruby, Tina, and the doctor joined them. They exchanged hugs with the two athletes. Perry Karas and Dr. Halle Berry-Look-Alike also exchanged a brief kiss, which evoked a rising hum and applause from the crowd. It ended with the exchange of smiles of affection between the two attractive young people.

"It's the lead, ladies and gentlemen," Lana said. "Henry has been struggling from the effects of the lead in Flint's drinking water. He has been getting the best care from Dr. Majors and others at the hospital, and Henry and all of us have great hopes for his complete recovery."

The boy gave Lana a weak smile and pumped a fist in the air.

"Henry will do the honors and draw the first of twenty-five names from this big hat. Those twenty-five will be asked to take on the vitally important job of turning your ideas into some fundamental changes to our state constitution. This will be a new landmark in the history of democracy, right here in our state. Henry, draw the first name, if you will."

On the large monitors around the room, a camera showed folded blue-and-green pieces of paper in the hat. Townsend and Karas helped Henry to his feet. Henry slowly bent over and reached into the hat. He handed a slip of paper to Lana.

"The first of our 'draftee drafters,'" announced Lana,

taking the slip from Henry, "is Percy Oliver from Lansing. Percy, are you here?"

Lamarcus and Perry helped Henry back into the wheelchair as a robust-looking African-American man raised his hand from the middle of the crowded room.

Lana waved him up.

As the man wove through the crowd, Angelo felt a mixture of envy and relief. Percy Oliver was all smiles as he bent to shake Henry's hand before greeting the others on the stage.

Lana said, "You are our historic first. Of course, we need all the help we can get from Lansing. If you don't mind, can you tell us what you do there?"

"I'm an associate professor of English at Michigan State," Oliver said.

There was a pause for photos. "Governor, can you join us?" Lana called out.

Charlie Birnbaum had been standing in the front row, a glass of tonic in his hand and a huge smile on his face. He took one athletic leap onto the stage, without spilling a drop of his drink. He joined Henry and Percy Oliver in the front of the group, then moved to the back for more photos.

"Twenty-four more names to announce," Lana said.

The group on the stage remained while Lana called twenty-four more people to each draw a name from the hat—mostly children, some hospitalized, some not; some with lead poisoning and possible brain damage; and a few adults who had suffered from Legionnaires' disease. Additional healthcare workers joined them led by the courageous Mona Hanna-Attisha, the Hurley pediatrician who was the first to expose the Flint water crisis.

Angelo's name was drawn near the end by a little girl

with long, straight, shiny, blonde hair. A path to the stage seemed to open. He was trembling as he approached the stage.

Only one other well-known person was picked—the newly elected state House Representative from Saginaw, Susan Kerns. The rest were, like Angelo, unknowns.

After all the names had been called, Lana congratulated the group before cautioning everyone about reports of ice conditions on the roads. "Please, make it home safely and thank you all so much."

CHAPTER 9

Ice

Angelo's head swirled with thoughts about the day's events as he pulled out of the parking ramp and headed with longing back to Lexi in their Best Western hotel room in Birch Run. He couldn't wait for the miles to be eaten up by his truck. He wanted to tell her about everything. He was now *in*, really *in*, his name drawn from the hat. Was he in over his head? Lexi would be happy, but was he?

As soon as he drove onto Interstate 75, he realized he was virtually driving on ice. Traffic barely moved. By the time he reached Auburn Hills, a normal trip of twenty minutes or so, he had been driving well over an hour. At this speed, it would take three hours for what should have been an easy hour to Flint, then it would be another forty-five minutes or so north to Birch Run.

The urban traffic thinned out the farther north he was from Detroit but it was still slow going on the ice, twenty to twenty-five miles per hour, sometimes coming to a full stop. He saw several cars that had slid off the road and one multi-car pileup. Blue lights were blinking but he kept going. When he saw the sign for an upcoming exit to Fenton, about thirty-five miles from Birch Run, he thought of pulling off and finding a hotel for the night. He spotted a pizza restaurant just before the exit and realized he was hungry too.

He was about to move into the right-hand lane to exit when he saw that a barely visible dark Ford had slid into the median to his left. A black woman stood next to the car, pulling her light jacket closely around her as she gingerly stepped closer to the highway. Taking care not to slide into the median himself, he slowed the truck to a stop to offer his assistance. Up close, he realized she was the mother of one of the kids that had drawn a name at Cobo. The look in her eyes revealed panic and she pleaded to him for help.

"I know you," she said. "I saw you on the stage, at Cobo. My daughter's in the back, with her nurse. We need to get back to Hurley as soon as possible. I knew she shouldn't have made the trip but she wanted to so badly— she wanted to be there with the other sick kids—I had to take her. Her doctor said it would be okay for this one special day. I hoped it would perk her up; she's been so sad. Can you get our car out of here? This is like a ditch."

Angelo tried to calm her before he got in her car and tried to drive it. The wheels were stuck deep in icy mud. He got out and told her to get everyone in his truck. He would drive them to the hospital and home.

"Bless you," she said.

The girl, Georgetta, was three. They got her car seat buckled into the backseat of Angelo's truck and everyone else squeezed in front.

At Hurley's emergency entrance, Angelo and the nurse helped the sleeping girl into a waiting wheelchair. He stayed while she was transferred to the Pediatric Center, where the nurse and another attendant placed Georgetta into her hospital bed. She immediately fell back asleep.

With assurances from the nurse that Georgetta was okay, Angelo and Etta returned to his truck. He drove Etta to her home, in a settled, comfortable-looking neighborhood of tidy houses.

"We'll get your car in the morning. I'm sure everything will be fine," Angelo said. Etta gave him a hug and he was on his way.

Before he got back onto the freeway, Angelo stopped and called Lexi. It was after midnight. She answered on the second ring.

"I've had the worst feelings. Please, tell me you're okay."

"I'm fine, but so much has happened." He told her about the trip to Flint. "And, Lex," he said, "there's something else. I got chosen to be in the constitutional-amendment-drafting group. I'm one of the twenty-five."

"I told you, didn't I? It's your time."

"I knew you would say that," he said. "I'm not so sure. I might not do it. I have the weekend to decide. Right now, I just want to get back to the hotel and to you and to our bed. I'm wiped out."

"Be safe."

At the hotel, Angelo slept deeply but not for long. He awoke early with his head buzzing about getting Etta's car taken care of. He made himself a cup of black coffee with the in-room coffee maker and then got into the shower while the drink cooled. By the time he finished in the bathroom, Lexi was already up and dressed in her jeans.

"Just give me time to put on a little makeup and I'll be ready to go."

They went to the breakfast room but only grabbed two bananas, bagels, and two more cups of black coffee to take in the truck. They were on the road by seven-thirty. The highway had been scraped and salted clear of ice; and, since it was a Saturday, there was little traffic. They reached the Fenton exit by eight.

Etta's car was still in the median. Lexi and Angelo placed the tarps and towels behind the wheels of the car to help get some traction in the semi-frozen ruts. Angelo attached the tow chain from his truck to the Ford and managed to pull the car free—muddy but otherwise okay. Lexi followed Angelo in Etta's car. Matters were moving along well this morning, he thought.

Etta was looking out a window when they pulled up to the house. She rushed out the door, looking drawn. She hugged Angelo again and smiled wanly at Lexi when Angelo introduced them.

"This man may have saved my daughter's life," she said. "I can't tell you both how thankful I am."

"Your car is fine," Lexi said.

"You heard about Henry, I suppose?" said Etta.

"Henry?" Lexi said.

"Henry Ortega," Etta said, "the boy who picked the first name out of the hat last night. The one who has been so sick and in the hospital. You didn't see it on the news?"

Angelo thought she was talking about coverage of the ceremony. He replied that they hadn't had a chance to see any news.

Etta shook her head. "Henry was killed in a big traffic pileup last night. Henry Ortega is dead."

CHAPTER 10

Free Press

As was his morning routine, Charlie Birnbaum let his dog, Hadley, out into to the backyard, got on his rowing machine for thirty minutes, brought the dog in, poured some food into her bowl, and made a pot of coffee for himself and Jacquie, who would soon be up. He picked up the day's edition of the *Detroit Free Press* from the porch of the governor's mansion—all while still in his pajamas and a robe. It was a chilly morning. Though cold, the sloppy weather of the night before had come to an end.

Other papers, like the *Lansing Journal, New York Times* and the *Washington Post*, would be waiting for him at his Capitol office, but his long standing habit was to start the day with coffee and the "Freep" at home in his comfortable recliner in the family room.

He was surprised to see a Jimmy Owens column across the top of the page. Primarily a sports writer for the paper, Owens' daily column was called "Time Out." In addition to being the paper's most popular columnist, he was also known beyond Michigan for two best-selling nonfiction books of sports nostalgia. On Sunday's, however, he wrote a column called "Owens' Opinions," which covered a wide range of subjects beyond sports. This was not a Sunday, but there it was across the top of the page:

Listening to Michigan Speak

Yesterday I was a proud citizen of the state of Michigan, something I haven't often been able to say in recent times, these troubled times in our state. When I say I was a citizen, that's just what I was. Not a journalist, not a reporter, not a columnist. I was one of 5,000 citizens participating in an event called "Michigan Speaks." This was phase one, I guess you could call it, of fulfilling Governor Charlie's promise of a new deck of cards for a new and different game, of creating a new framework for doing the state government's business.

Owens summarized the makeup of the group of people and the process of the meeting. What he expected was chaos. What he witnessed was something quite different.

My expectations were not high. Throw that many Michigan residents together—in these days in particular—into a huge room to plan a future for the state and the result would have to be like one of those comic firing squads, all in a circle shooting at the victim in the center. Like that, only on a huge scale. Five thousand shooters all pointed at each other—yelling at each other all the while, full of self-righteousness, full of anger, full of curses and complaints, full of fury. The only thing that could save them would be if the countdown to fire collapsed into chaos and they gave up and went home.

Instead, nothing like that happened.

The discussions at my table of ten were vigorous yet respectful of different points of view. I met and worked with people I don't get to see or talk to every day: a farmer from Bad Axe; a UAW shop steward from Ford Sterling Heights; a teacher from Saginaw; a Muslim father and small-business owner from Dearborn; a high-tech programmer from Troy; a Yooper policewoman from Marquette; a retired pharmacist from Farmington who now lives near Traverse City; a high school football coach from Fowlerville; a UPS manager from Grand Rapids; and me, your lovable, ink-stained wretch. These folks were serious, even earnest, in their views; and concerned about the past, present, and future of our state.

Naturally, we didn't all see things the same way. These were all nice folks, mind you. None of them were patsies. But at the end of the day, five thousand people were enthusiastic over the results.

That Brahmin conservative, William Buckley, once said, "I'd rather entrust the government of the United state to the first 400 people listed in the Boston telephone directory than to the faculty of Harvard University." Fair enough. I'd rather entrust the government of the state of Michigan to the people in that room yesterday, than to the members of the Michigan state House or Senate, and of course, to our most recent ex-governor, Old Stonehead.

During the wrap-up happy hour, they pushed the reset button by literally DRAWING NAMES FROM A HAT. They pulled twenty-five names to begin the process of drafting amendment(s) based on the output from this first session.

Henry Ortega, a teenager suffering from the lead contamination in Flint's drinking water, drew the first name: MSU professor Percy Oliver. More Flint kids, as well as a few adults who were recovering from Legionnaires' disease, chose the rest. A ceremony that even moved this hardened scribe.

When I got to the newsroom last night to write this column, one of my colleagues asked how the big meeting at Cobo went. My answer was simple: "Democracy, baby. It was democracy."

Charlie couldn't stop smiling as he read. Then his eyes were caught by a shaded box at the bottom of the page.

Boy Killed in Icy Crash after Conference

Riding home to Flint, from the conference at Cobo

Hall, in his family's car, fourteen-year-old Henry Ortega was killed on icy I-75 in a multi-car accident.

Birnbaum dropped the paper onto his lap and looked up in disbelief as his wife walked into the room.

"What is it, Charlie?" Jacquie said. "You look like you're in shock."

"The boy from Flint who pulled the first name from the hat last night ..." He read the headline and lead sentence aloud to his wife.

"Oh, no. How in the world ...?"

"I haven't read the rest. I'm not sure I want to."

It was a seven-car crash. The boy was killed. His sister suffered minor injuries. The mother was being treated for shock. All were wearing seatbelts.

Jacquie said it was beyond belief. She took his hand in both of hers. "Keep reading. I'll get you a fresh cup of coffee."

Charlie put the paper down again and simply stared out the window into the backyard before turning once again to read. There were few details. The story must have been added at the last moment before the paper went to press. With some reluctance, he read the main story about the conference, which did not mention the accident.

It was pretty much straight reporting on the process and outcomes, on the whole mostly favorable coverage, crediting the governor for following through on campaign promises, commenting on the democratic nature of the conference, the serious and active participation of the people, and the drawing of the names from the hat.

Charlie handed the paper to Jacquie when she returned with the coffee.

"Look at Jimmy Owens' column."

He paced as she read.

"Well, this is wonderful, isn't it?" she said.

"Could have been." He put his mug down and the two of them embraced.

Later, while he was upstairs getting dressed, his phone rang.

"It's Lana," he said.

CHAPTER 11

The Funeral

The email popped up on Angelo's phone while he and Lexi were eating lunch at a popular Flint-area eatery, Angelo's Famous Coney Island, and watching the scroll under the local news on the muted monitor: "5,000 citizens at Cobo, 25 names pulled from a hat. Henry Ortega's tragic death."

"What now?" Angelo said as he reached for his phone.

From: Lana Hartman
Subject: Henry Ortega
Date: January 14, 2019, 9:27:01 AM EDT
To: Angelo RoundSky and 5,012 more

I am sending this email to all five thousand of you who participated in our Michigan Speaks conference. I am also posting it on our Facebook and Twitter pages.

She broke the news, which was anything but to Angelo and Lexi.

> Henry's funeral will be held at
> Our Lady of Guadalupe Catholic
> Church in Flint this Tuesday at
> 10:30 a.m. All are invited to the
> funeral. If you can't attend,
> please keep Henry, his mother
> Ruby, and his sister Tina, in your
> thoughts and prayers.

Angelo and Lexi arrived early for the funeral mass and sat in the second row. Seated in the front pew with Henry's mother and sister were Perry Karas and Dr. Julia Majors, Lamarcus Townsend, Lana, and Governor and Mrs. Birnbaum. Soon the church overflowed to standing room only, with some people having to be shunted off to another room to listen over the PA system. It looked like the entire Hispanic community of greater Flint was there. The governor had been asked to speak, but he politely declined out of concern that it might appear to politicize the solemn service.

Angelo could follow everything as the service shifted between English and Spanish. The presiding priest delivered a moving and personalized homily for Henry, turning near the end to an eloquent condemnation of the human-inflicted blunders that brought Henry and the whole city to this sad point. Finally, he made a plea for human forgiveness. "As difficult as that may be." He asked those assembled to pray for the new governor, that he might do his best to insure nothing like the Flint health crisis ever happened again.

When he finished, twelve-year-old Tina slowly rose from her seat next to her mother and walked to the altar.

She was obviously nervous as she began to speak, barely visible behind the lectern. Some people were crying before she uttered a word.

"Like all big brothers, I guess, my brother, Henry, was a pest. He loved to tease me, and I pretended to hate him for it, but I always knew he did it because he cared about me, because he loved me. He always stuck up for me if other people were mean to me, even sometimes if it was our mom. And then, the next minute, he would be mocking me or making fun of me.

"I hated it when he got lead sick. He tried to still be my protector but I knew he couldn't even protect himself. He got so weak when he was in the hospital, he seemed like he wanted me to take charge, to help our mom. He seemed to know that he wouldn't be able to do that anymore. And his teasing sometimes wasn't just for fun anymore. Sometimes he really got mad at anything and everything, including me. I think it was just because he hurt a lot.

"His body was hurting, and so was his heart. He tried so hard and fought so hard. He could always do everything better than anybody else—baseball, soccer, football, Ping Pong, and his favorite, basketball. And he was really smart in school. But his body and his brain wouldn't let him do those things anymore. He hated that and it made him mad and sometimes he got mad at me.

"But now it was my turn. Now I had to be his *protector and I tried, but in the end, I couldn't do it. I loved my brother but I couldn't stop that accident and I couldn't stop the thing that really took him away from us even*

before that accident—the lead in the water. My big brother was my hero and he knew it. He also knew he couldn't be the kind of hero he wanted to be for me and my mom anymore.

"But right now, I want to tell him and I want everybody else to know too—Henry, you are still and always will be my big-brother hero."

Tina could barely get through her last sentence. She had to stop after almost every word and recompose herself but finally got to the last word and walked back to her seat with her head in her hands hiding her tears.

Angelo saw Perry looking over Dr. Major's head toward Lamarcus, whose head was down, one hand on his forehead. Perry reached over her shoulder to nudge him. Angelo could hear Lamarcus whisper as quietly as he could: "You go, man. I'm too fucking mad right now. Don't nobody let me up there. You go. You do it."

Perry shrugged and slowly stood. He bent to Tina and Ruby, and took their hands, quietly asking them to join him on the altar. They hesitated but did join Perry on the short walk to the lectern. He announced that he and Lamarcus were establishing an initiative called "Henry's Helpers" to raise money to help Henry's family as well as other victims and the families of those victims. "We will be working in cooperation with many other groups that are doing so much in this city already." He and Lamarcus were each donating $1 million as seed money.

He ended with, "Tina, your brother would be so proud of you this morning. You are our hero today. God bless you and your mom. Henry will never be forgotten."

People left the service with grief, anger, and, thanks to

Perry and Lamarcus, motivated to act. Angelo had been angry since he first heard the news about Henry, and it only grew as the funeral service went on. Now, standing outside the church, blinking in the bright sunlight, he took Lexi by the hand and said under his breath, "Let's get the hell out of here."

He was silent once they were headed north on I-75. Lexi knew earlier, when Angelo unexpectedly checked them out of their Birch Run hotel, that something was up. He was fed up, he said. He would come back to help in the future, but right now he needed to get away. So now, on the road, she didn't bother him.

When they came to the first rest stop, Angelo pulled in. They hadn't been to the bathroom since before the funeral. Lexi's first words when he stopped were, "Thank, god." This elicited a little smile and a pat on the hand from her man.

"You drive," he said when they returned to the car.

"You sure?"

"Yes. I didn't get any sleep at all last night, I don't think," he said.

She got behind the wheel, told him to take it easy. He was still feeling the anger, arguing with himself and others. Sleep would not come easily. After a few minutes, his eyes seemed to pop open of their own accord. It was probably useless to keep on trying but was he happy to let Lexi continue driving.

"I'm going to do it," he finally said.

"Do what?"

"That twenty-five man drafting committee or whatever it's called."

"It's not a twenty-five-man anything when almost half are women."

"You know what I mean."

She laughed. "That's the problem with guys. They act like men do everything of importance. I can't believe you would even consider *not* doing it. It may be the biggest chance of your life."

"I know I need to do it. For Henry, if for no other reason. And, I know there are lots of other reasons." He paused and looked out at the flat farmland. "But I have to do something else first."

"I think I know."

"North Manitou. I need to try again."

"That was my guess. I think you *should*. But in late January? Are you sure this is the right time?"

"Probably not. But I must do it before the meetings start."

"You do what you have to. You know how to survive outside in the cold."

"I think I do, Lex. And, I need to do this now."

CHAPTER 12

The Names in the Hat

From: Lana Hartman
Subject: The Names in the Hat
Date: January 21, 2019 10:12 AM
To: Michigan Constitution Council
Members

Below you will find the names and
home locations of the twenty-five
people whose names were drawn to
be the drafters of a new constitution for our state. Our first
group meeting will be held on the
last weekend in February, beginning with a reception and dinner
on Friday, February 22, and con-
clude with lunch on Sunday, February 24, 2019. The location will be
the Riverfront Center on the Flint
U of M campus. We will honor Henry
Ortega at the opening dinner.

You will see an asterisk next to
three of the names listed below.

These names were drawn to replace three of the original draftees who, for various reasons, cannot participate. These new members were among the five thousand at the Cobo conference. Their names were drawn from the same hat as everyone else's. We are happy that they will join us in this vitally important endeavor.

We look forward to getting started soon. See all of you in Flint.

Names	Home Location
Jesse Anselmo	Gaylord
Morris Balzer	Jackson
Harold Marshall	Detroit
Richard Berger	Grosse Pointe
Lauren Bommarito	Grand Rapids
James "Buzz" Boyer	Ludington
Boyd Carl	Wyandotte
Dale Darcy	Ypsilanti
Madeline Edges*	Chelsea
Paul Ernesto	Albion
Perry Karas	Troy
Wayne Keith	St. Louis
Susan Kerns	Saginaw
Nicholas Lahti	Houghton
Bradley May*	Midland
Marsha Norway	Escanaba
Percy Oliver	Okemos
Marta Orosco	Hart
Cher Richie	Dearborn
Holly Rifkin	Beverly Hills
Thomas Samuels*	Bad Axe
Angelo RoundSky	Eagletown
Martha Smith	Flint
Wynn Stewbie	Bloomfield Hills
Lemuel Tracker	Mt. Pleasant

CHAPTER 13

Preparing for Passage

The biggest obstacle Angelo faced as he prepared for his trip to North Manitou was the weather. He packed as though he were going deer hunting for a week in the UP in late November, something he had done many times before. Two key differences: he would be making this trip alone and he would not be taking any food. Moreover, while the weather during hunting season could be very cold, by late January into early February, the Lake Michigan waters would have turned from cold to frigid, sometimes even completely icing over. His greatest threat would be hypothermia. And there was always the possibility of the strong northwest winds, a Canadian Clipper, and lake-effect snow. It was crazy to go on the island this time of year. He knew the risks. He knew.

On the other hand, Angelo had always been tempted by the challenge of making the eight-mile crossing on ice. He had heard tales. He was curious to try it. And there was the matter of a deadline.

Regardless of his earlier doubts and hesitations, his conviction and commitment to play whatever part he could in the rewriting of the constitution had taken hold deep within. It would be easier to delay his quest until May, when the island ferry service would be running and the weather would be warmer, but he had received Lana Hartman's email and knew he had no time to spare. He needed to get himself ready for the passage, now.

Lexi helped Angelo plan in earnest. They monitored the weather forecasts and hoped for a break between winter storms. The winter of 2018/19 was one of the most severe with temperatures frequently below zero, polar vortices, and severe lake-effect snowfalls. One aspect of the bad news, however, was actually good news for Angelo: the thick ice coverage on Lake Michigan would allow him to hike the eight miles from Glen Haven to the southwest shore of North Manitou island. The second week of February appeared to be his best shot. A warm spell in the twenties, with light southwest winds, was predicted.

Lexi prepared a detailed checklist of supplies and made sure their sex life was as full as their other preparations. The weekend of February 15 looked as good as they could hope for, allowing them to enjoy a special Valentine's Day.

Lexi prayed to the Great Spirit of Manitou that Angelo would fulfill his quest sooner rather than later. He promised to return no later than Monday, February 18. If nothing had happened by then, he would just get on with his life without it.

Grandmother Emma thought the whole idea was crazy. She said, "Maybe your drunken father knew what he was talking about when you tried this as boy. Maybe it's all just Indian bullshit."

"Maybe he was," Angelo said.

Lexi agreed with Grandma but kept her counter arguments to herself and continued to help Angelo prepare. And she stayed busy with her job; anything to avoid thinking about the worst.

At first light on the morning of the 15th, the three of them made their way to Glen Haven, a sled full of supplies in the back of the truck. The two women held Angelo as long as they could before he pulled himself loose to tread out onto the ice, pulling a sled filled with ice picks, ropes, and changes of warm clothes in case he fell through a patch of thin ice. For shelter he had a tent, a sleeping bag, thermal blankets, and a propane stove for heat, since he would not be cooking any food.

Ahead of him, all he saw was jagged ice caused by the cycles of freezing and thawing and refreezing. He looked back to see the two women holding each other. He knew they would drive to his grandmother's house, where Lexi planned to stay until he returned home. They said they didn't want to worry alone.

He turned and began his journey.

CHAPTER 14

Manitou Passage

2/15/19 Friday

It's not easy writing in this little red journal you gave me. My cold stiff fingers don't work so good. Hope we can read my writing when I get back.

I am keeping this log for you, Lex, so you will have a record in case anything happens to me. I don't plan on anything bad happening, but who knows? If I end up OK, I also want to have this log for my own sake—a record I can look back on. Also, of course, for my grandmother.

Right now, I'm tired but excited. I made it across the ice OK.

It was a rugged start with the jagged ice and all. Not for long though. After a short distance, it smoothed out. All I had to look out for was thin ice. I checked every little while but it was solid all the way and walking was not too hard. The Crib lighthouse was awesome. Kind of eerie walking up to it in the middle of Lake Michigan. Using my ice pick, I managed to climb to the top of the base. I wanted a good view of my route. Sure enough, I could see a road of smooth ice all the way to the island. Other routes looked much more rugged. Near the shore it got rough again, but beautiful with ice cliffs and ice caves.

I didn't take much time to explore. I was just happy to be on land. Took me about 4 hrs. Once on shore, I rested up and looked back at what I had just done. Tired but still pumped up.

I took off my backpack and ice spikes and hid the sled (Who from? I don't know.) under some brush. The main west trail, which I have been on before, was covered in snow and hard to see at times. All the hardwoods are mostly bare except for a few leftover brown leaves on some of the oaks. The pines have some green left to them. The shrubbery and wild grasses are also dead and brown. It was cold but I was plenty warm in my thermals. Sweating some, in fact. I passed the old Swenson's barn area, walking until shortly before sunset. You should see this winter sunset over the big lake. It was a mostly cloudy day, but it cleared tonight just above the horizon and there was a gap for the sun. The clouds turned from deep-red and orange to pink and purple and blue.

Once I got my camp set up, I tried my phone. No signal. Maybe it will be better in the daytime.

I'm hungry. The camp stove helps some for the heat but I AM HUNGRY. Part of what it's all about, right?

No visions or spirit visits. Not even many animals about—I guess they're smarter than me. I did see two foxes in the woods together. A bald eagle flew overhead. None of them stopped to talk to me though. LOL.

My camp is set for the night. The air mattress will keep me off the ground. I'm going commando in my sleeping bag so my clothes don't sweat and freeze. Tomorrow I'll hike to the bluffs.

I am happy because I know your spirit is with me even if the manitou hasn't found me yet. More tomorrow.

2/16/19 Saturday

7:30 a.m. It feels late but it's still pitch dark. Thanks for the new 4-season tent. It kept me warm last night. I boiled some water before settling in. Poured it in a water bottle and slipped it inside the bag long enough to warm it up. Cozy.

I'm about to be on the road toward the bluffs. Same sort of weather as yesterday, but clouds forming in the west. No storms forecast but not looking good right now.

Noon: stopped for a rest and checked radio forecast again. Squall may be headed this way. Changing my plans. Will head to Lake Manitou in the middle of the island. It's at a lower level. Snows may just blow over the top of the dunes. If it's bad and snows through tomorrow, I may have to just hunker down until I head back. Don't want to do that. That's not what I came for. But can't beat nature. Maybe that's the secret the Great Spirit has for me. Go with the flow, Angelo.

I'm hungry.

3 p.m. Made it to Lake Manitou. Sky still looking like a squall line headed this way. A few small flakes so far, and stronger winds from the northwest. Nothing too bad. Lake Manitou is a beautiful little lake. Glad I got to see it again.

Not hungry anymore. Past that stage but feeling a little light-headed. I'm happy about where I am and what I'm trying to do, but I can't say I feel good. After setting up camp again, I'll take a walk around the lake. Don't want to try to sleep too soon.

4:30. Saw some fish under the ice in the shallows—

trout or smallmouth. Spotted another fox or two. Are they following me? Or should I follow them? What if they're the manitou? Do they want me to do something? I tried talking to them but they just trotted off—like foxes.

Doesn't take long to walk around this lake. Reminds me of Banff and Lake Louise. Remember how surprised we were when we walked around Lake Louise? Wish you could see this one and walk around it with me.

A problem. My propane stove is not working. I've been fussing with it since I got back. Maybe my brain isn't working at this stage. I'll have to find enough wood and kindling to build a fire. It's against the park rules but who's going to catch me? I'll be careful and clean up after I put it out. Wind squalls could be a problem if I'm wrong about it blowing over the top. Wet snow, too, but not expecting wet snow.

The snow is not too bad for walking, not deep—haven't needed my snowshoes yet—just those spikes that slip on over my shoes—but everything is pretty damp for lighting fires. Finally got one going. Will be able to heat the sleeping bag with the water bottle again. Just hope my camp doesn't get buried in a blizzard or something. No sunset to brag about tonite, though. I'm sure of that.

5:30. Snow coming down steady but no blizzard yet. Wind is up again but I'm protected from it down here. Got some rocks together to put on the fire and placed some medicine ties with tobacco, cedar, sage and sweetgrass in the fire too. Can't hurt. Trying to remember what the elders did back in the day, but my mind is foggy.

I don't want to go to sleep too early, but after dark there isn't much else I can do around here. I'm so damned tired I wouldn't want to do it if I could. Plus my head feels thick and useless. Trying not to think about food. Trying not to think about anything. Stay warm and get ready for a good night's sleep.

As I'm writing this, a big bald eagle flew over. It seemed to look down at me, looked me right in the eye and I stared back at him. I <u>think</u> that's what happened. I'm not sure of anything. I don't know what tonite and tomorrow will be like.

After midnight. The wind is howling over the top of my tent. It's so loud it woke me up. I'm protected but it sounds like it could blow my tent away. The snow is beating on the tent fast. Maybe it's sleet. I'm cold and getting a <u>little</u> worried.

2/17/17 Sunday

7:30 a.m. Crazy sleep last night. Lots of crazy, restless dreams I can't remember. Slept pretty well all thru the nite even with the twists and turns. Then I woke up to a miracle. No, not like that. Still no spirits. But the weather cleared overnight. It's now colder than hell. Below zero I'm sure and i'm having trouble wrtg this. But it's clear as bell. Calm.

Everything looks and smells fresh. Snow deeper though. Can't say I'm clear as the weather. My head is a bit foggy. My legs feel like lead. Must be the fasting. Need to get a move on. Probably leave camp set up here for tonight. I'm headed out for the bluffs now.

My plan is to pack up and head home tomorrow. For sure I'm missing you (and a hot meal). Eagle flew over again just now—looking down at me again. What's he want? Am I his lunch or is he my manitou?

4:30 p.m. Lex, it's been quite a day. After my time on the bluff, I came back down to Lake Manitou—down, down, down; way, way, way down—can't begin to tell you. Just sat at my camp for an hour or so meditating or something. Maybe just stunned.

Then I packed up and took the old railroad bed back here to the south end to get an early start home tomorrow. I should be exhausted but my adrenaline's got me so high I could make it back to Glen Haven right now—and I want to—I want to share this day with you.

Later—

How could I sleep? Don't know if I should say anything else now. If I tell you, you'll think I'm crazy. Not sure about any of it myself.

This is about how it started. It's all good. So good!

It was a struggle to get to the top of the bluff. I had to use my snowshoes. In the cold, with the shape I'm in, it was hard labor. Like climbing up Sleeping Bear Dunes from Lake Michigan but more gullies and such. But once I got up to the bluffs it was like standing on top of the Bear trying to see Wisconsin.

Except for this!!!!!!

Are eagles supposed to be around here this time of year? There they were—way below me. Three of them standing down on the ice of Lake Michigan. Except for turning their heads now and then, they were just standing there still, each one looking off in a different direction, north, south, and east.

Then I saw a fourth eagle in the water, a little pool of open water, facing west.

The four winds.

At first I thought it was a duck or a goose, but there it was—a big, old bald eagle just floating there like a duck in a fair-size opening in the ice.

That's when it happened. Waiting to tell you the rest tomorrow.

Much later. Still can't sleep. I have to write down the rest of this.

Four eagles, three standing on the ice and the one in water, facing in the directions of the four winds. All of a sudden, without any sort of signal I could detect, the three on the ice took off, each in its own direction. I spun around, tried to follow each as far as I could. Then I looked down at the eagle in the water.

He started swimming—away from the shore—to the west. Then it rose enough to shake its wings, settled back down, and seemed to turn its head back toward me just before he lifted into the air and flew to the west. It flew, it soared, it swooped back my way, all the way back to me, looking right at me and signaling me with his head. It scared me. I was afraid he would grab me in his talons. He got so close and without thinking I leaped on its back. We took off together, headed west again, headed for you know where—Wisconsin. But all the time we kept rising and rising and rising—my ears filled with the whooshing of his wings and whooshing of air as we rose fast as a jet it seemed.

And then we were OVER Wisconsin, OVER it!!!! I looked

down on the waters of Green Bay and the Door County peninsula and then farmland. Then we flew even higher and higher.

When I looked up, I didn't see blue sky anymore. All I could see was black, like outer space. When I looked down, I could see the curvature of the earth and a hundred miles or two in each direction.

Behind me, the earth curved back over the lake to Michigan, the mitten and the UP. I thought of you down there and Grandma Emma and Dad, wherever he is or if he is. And your brother Mark. I thought of Henry and the 5000 and the 25 from the hat. Then we flew farther and faster, swooping this way and that, lower then higher again, looking west and south and north, over the whole of North America up to the Arctic and down over to Europe and Asia and the Himalayas and over other mountains, oceans, and the deserts and the forests and south over Africa and the mountains and deserts and rivers and canals and over Antarctica and Australia and the deserts and the Pacific and island chains and the volcanoes and rivers and forests and the ... everything and everyplace ... swooping and rising and falling and rising. I couldn't distinguish the countries. There were no borders.

And then falling, falling through space, coming closer and closer to the earth until I could see Michigan, waves of the lake, over the Sleeping Bear and her two cubs, until finally the eagle set me down on a huge rock on the bluffs of North Manitou and flew away. I stood there. On the bluffs. On that rock. Alone. The eagle flew west until it was out of sight.

I stood there, feeling all new. Feeling the curvature of the earth under my feet. Feeling myself standing in just that one spot but also standing on the surface of the earth as a whole, not standing on the edge of it so much as mingling with it. Only feeling. No words. I'm standing on the world, feeling its giant roundness under my feet. Feeling all the great oceans and all the great land masses, the mountains and the deserts. The whole planet at my feet and all around me.

Seeing all the way to Wisconsin was not the point any more.

CHAPTER 15

Return Passage

Angelo woke the next morning warm in his sleeping bag—almost too warm. A second consecutive day of clear skies and a mild southwest wind. He had to get on the move. There might already be some melting.

He left what equipment he could do without, doing his best to dispose of it carefully, to leave the island as close as he could to the way he found it.

Soon after he started out, he realized the trip home would be harder and slower than his trip over. He would have to take care to avoid thin or even nonexistent ice. Tired and hungry, hanging on mentally as best he could, he had little time to reflect on the thrill of the day before. That adrenaline rush was gone. *This is the reality of reality,* he thought. *Back to business.* He concentrated on Lexi and home, and smiled to think he still had his old stubbornness to get him there.

A few hours into his walk, as he got closer to the Glen Haven shoreline, he got a signal on his cell, so he called Lexi to let her know he was safe and would be there shortly. All along he had been writing in his log as though he was talking directly to her, but she had heard nothing from him until that phone call. She said she was worried and she missed him. She didn't want him to hang up. She said she wanted to hear all about his trip, didn't want to wait. Angelo asked her to be patient; it was a long story. He wanted to share it with her in person. Plus, he was too busy to talk. He had choppy or melted ice and flowing water to avoid while pulling his sled.

Lexi and Angelo's grandmother were there to meet him when he pulled his lightened sled up on shore. The two women were all about hugs and tears, while Angelo was more reflective and quiet—happy to be home but still in another mysterious space. He asked Lexi to drive the truck. He was tired from the crossing. He said, "Take Grandma home first, okay?"

On the way to Grandma Emma's, Angelo shared the basics—the crossing each way, his camp, the trails, the threatening weather followed by the surprisingly sunny and benign day. He mentioned animals and a little about the one eagle flying overhead. He told it all as economically as he could, with almost no emotion. He wanted to be nice to his grandmother without giving away anything of real importance. When they reached her house, she invited them in, but he begged off, using his exhaustion and hunger as an excuse to get home.

When they finally arrived at their place, Lexi was all over him, physically and verbally. She peppered him with questions. He begged for some time to rest, saying only that it was an amazing experience; that this time it was for real.

As she tucked him into bed, he said, "Yes. My answer is yes."

"You mean it?" she almost screamed. "You mean it?" Dammit, I told you next time you were going to have to do the proposing. Now, you just say yes and get me all stirred up."

"I mean it," he said. He handed her the journal, which was really just a long letter to her. "Now, read this. When I wake up we'll talk. Let me nap and then I'll fill in the rest." He patted her back as they embraced. "It may not feel fair to you, asking you to wait, but I want to be fully there with you when we talk about it. I just can't do that right now."

"Damn you. And if you're *asking*, my answer is yes. Now, get some sleep so I can have all of you here with me. That's all I really want anyway. Well, that and the rest of your story."

When Angelo woke, it dawned on him that he had not had a shower in days. He reveled in the warm water as it splashed over him and thought of Lexi and what he had written. He was unsure of what her reaction might be. Would she think he had lost his mind? How could she even understand, let alone feel anything like what he had felt? But, if anyone could even come close, she could. Of that he was sure.

Lexi heard him in the shower and took a cold beer in an iced mug into their bedroom. His knees almost buckled when he saw her in a long, sheer, white-lace negligee that contrasted with as well as revealed her silky olive skin. Her black eyes flashed.

Naked, he could not conceal his response.

She laughed. "I went shopping while you were gone."

Later, back in her negligee, she went into the kitchen and returned to their bed with some starchy, salty snacks to break his fast before the big meal she had planned. "I called your grandmother," she said.

"Yeah?"

"I told her we were going to get married. I couldn't help it. You were sleeping. I had to tell somebody. I have just been so excited."

"What did she say?" Angelo asked.

"She said it was about time."

"Sure. Did you expect anything else?"

"I just had to tell somebody. Now, let's get down to business. I mean, what the hell?!"

"Did you read the journal?"

"Of course, I read the journal. It was amazing. Real. But ..."

"But am I a crazy Indian?"

"That's not what I was going to say, but since you brought it up."

"Maybe I am. It seems crazy to me now, but it was as real as you are now when it happened."

"It probably *did* happen, just like you wrote it."

"Lex, I'm telling you, it was amazing. Now that I've had some sleep and a little bit to eat, I can almost feel it all over again. I saw the whole earth from what felt like outer space."

"All the cities and towns, all the people?"

"All I saw was the earth, the planet, the land and the waters and the sky. I saw trees and other vegetation. Not people or cities."

She waited while he took a long drink of beer. He put

his head back and closed his eyes. *Hard to describe*, he thought. *Unreal. But the most real thing he had ever experienced.*

She said, "Is that it?"

"Isn't that enough?"

"Amazing. Awesome. Wonderful, scary, and mind-boggling."

"All those things. I'm finished with the story, but I don't think it's finished with me."

"What do you think it all means?"

"No idea. Yet. I wasn't thinking, I was just feeling and experiencing. I'll be sorting it all out for the rest of my life—for the rest of our lives, that is."

"Let me help, if I can, please."

"You will, I know. We have the rest of our lives together to figure it out. I *do* know one thing." He tossed a handful of nuts in his mouth, took another drink. "I don't know for sure if it really happened or if I was just hallucinating from hunger and cold, but ..."

"But?"

"Oh, it doesn't matter."

"It doesn't *matter*?"

"All I know, for sure, is that it happened to *me*."

CHAPTER 16

Constitutional Council

The first meeting of the Constitutional Council took place in Flint's Riverfront Center, overlooking the waterway that was at the center of the lead-contamination crisis. At the opening-night cocktail party, Angelo and the other members of the Council were somber when they took their seats for dinner at five round tables. At one table, sat the Republican House Minority Leader Thom Jarrett and the Democratic Speaker of the House Janice Rison. Angelo was moved to see Ruby and Tina Ortega there, seated between the Governor and Lana.

Along with the council members, at the other tables were three news reporters, two from the Detroit papers and one from the *Lansing State Journal*. A television reporter stood by with a cameraman.

Lana called for their attention from a small lectern on a table at one end of the room. "We are so pleased to bring this group of citizens together from across our state to take on such an important challenge. You were chosen the way you were—out of a hat—because that's what we're all about: a democracy at work on the ills of democracy.

"Tomorrow you will get down to work in earnest.

Tonight, we only want to accomplish a couple things. Most importantly, we want to honor the all-too-short life of Henry Ortega, a young man who has been an inspiration to us all. Henry's mother and sister rose from their seats and were recognized and applauded.

Next, Lana motioned to Percy Oliver. She said, "Percy's was the first name drawn, pulled from the hat by Henry. He asked if he could say a few words before we all observe a moment of silence in Henry's name."

Percy stood up. "When Henry pulled my name out of that hat, he became a part of me. You know I'm from Okemos. I'm a Michigan State sports fan. I understand Henry was quite a good athlete. I'm on the Faculty Athletic Council at State, although I'm just a Poor Old English Teacher, that's P.O.E.T. I find my inspiration in literature—so, in memory of Henry Ortega, let me share a few lines of a classic poem by A.E. Housman. It's called 'To an Athlete Dying Young" and it speaks to the effects of his life and death on his community. Here are the first two stanzas:

> *The time you won your town the race*
> *We chaired you through the marketplace;*
> *Man and boy stood cheering by,*
> *And home we brought you shoulder-high.*
>
> *Today, the road all runners come,*
> *Shoulder-high we bring you home,*
> *And set you at your threshold down,*
> *Townsman of a stiller town.*

The group observed a moment of silence before quietly beginning to eat. At Angelo's table, the *Lansing Journal* reporter quizzed the members about what they thought of their undertaking. Aside from sober expressions of its importance and the earnest but humble commitment to their mission, it remained a friendly, if superficial, discussion. Angelo remained quiet, contributing only when the conversation centered on Henry Ortega or the Flint water crisis. With restrained but clear conviction, he spoke of the many other water-related issues facing the state. Perhaps for the first time in his life, he almost felt like one of the group.

Angelo could see that things were not so simple for Perry Karas. Perry was the one member everyone wanted to engage. "How is your health?" "How much longer?" "What about the playoffs? Will you be back?" "What do you think of the Wings' chances?" "How old were you (where were you) when you started playing?" Perry tried to steer the conversation back to the sick kids at Hurley. He spoke of his feelings about democracy. While polite, they gave little sign of actually listening and quickly turned back to hockey and sports talk.

After dinner, the Governor thanked the participants for their willingness to work on such a vital project and reiterated his support for their efforts. "I don't want to interfere," he said. "But I *do* want to help when I can. I am a hurdler, as you have heard."

Next, he thanked the two legislators for their presence and support. He explained that neither he nor they would stay for the weekend session, emphasizing his confidence in the democratic process and "you the people." He pointed to Susan Kerns, recently elected state House

Representative from Saginaw. "She will be here," he said, "not because she's a politician but because, just like the rest of you, her name was drawn from the hat."

He sat down to polite applause. Lana then announced a twenty-minute break before the council would reconvene in the adjacent room for its first official meeting.

CHAPTER 17

Why Are We Here?

"There it is," Perry Karas said to Angelo as they strolled to the main meeting room. One side of the hallway they were in was all glass. "The infamous Flint River."

"It's not the river's fault," said Angelo. He looked out into the dark night. He saw the lights of the Riverfront Center reflecting on the water, the lights of downtown Flint beyond, and the headlights of a few cars that slowly moved through the mostly empty streets.

He took a seat next to Perry at one of the tables, rectangles arranged in a square with space in the middle. Lana sat on Perry's other side. It pleased Angelo to think of himself as one of the three jocks in the group. A copy of the results from Michigan Speaks was at each place, with a list of the twenty-five names. While Perry and Lana chatted, Angelo leafed through the papers in the folder. He read: "Of the people, by the people, for the people." *We'll see*, he thought.

Lana rapped on the table with her knuckles and opened the meeting with another message about the opportunity and challenges facing the group. "After tonight, neither Governor Birnbaum nor I will be here with you. You

111111111111111111111

1111

will lead yourselves and establish whatever structure you think you need. Remember, while you are the chosen few, openness is important, both for the quality of the product—a new and better governance system; what the governor refers to as 'a new game'—and for the ultimate buy-in of that product by the people of this state. Historically, constitutions have been written by a small and often secret group, the US Constitution included. Governor Birnbaum believes he was elected by a large majority with a mandate to change that to "We, *all* the people" by engaging *all* the people in this process.

"Please try to honor the governor and that belief by opening up your process for suggestions and feedback from people throughout the state by whatever means you can create. Meet in closed sessions as needed, but we are prepared to livestream, podcast, and videotape meetings to be posted online. As you work, each new draft of any amendments will be posted online. Citizen input will be encouraged through Twitter, Facebook, email, and regular mail. Your work will not always be comfortable. It's called democracy, folks."

"Being comfortable is overrated," Perry said. "Sometimes you have to be uncomfortable to achieve something worthwhile."

Lana continued. "Tonight your only job is to get acquainted. I will join you this one time because I want to get to know you better. I want you to know me better as well. I will always be available to help if you need me, so it may be good if you get to know your hired help."

"Percy got us started already in the other room, thank you. Now, let's go around the room, starting to Percy's right, and introduce ourselves. And, don't worry, we don't expect poetry from the rest of you. Just briefly tell us a little about yourself and what you are thinking about our mission."

A smartly dressed black woman sitting next to Percy introduced herself as Martha Smith from Flint. She said she knew Percy from high-school days at Flint Central. She was now the Curriculum Director for the Flint Public Schools. "I doubt if I have to say anything more about how much this initiative means to me and this city. I also want to thank Lana and Governor Birnbaum for holding this first meeting in Flint. And, God bless Henry." She smiled and nodded to the next person.

There were two more educators: Wayne Keith, a high school principal for over twenty years from St. Louis; and Susan Kerns, a former grade-school teacher from Saginaw, author of two books of local history, and also the lead fundraiser for the local history museum. As the governor said earlier, Susan was recently elected to the state House of Representatives.

Madeline Edges and Thomas Samuels had been added to replace two people who had withdrawn their names. Mrs. Edges once owned Edges Books, a chain of over 400 stores across North America. The company went under a few years ago, and now Madeline lived in comfortable retirement in "my dear town of Chelsea, near Ann Arbor, where my business was based." Samuels was a West Point graduate, with a PhD in civil engineering from Purdue. A retired Army colonel, he returned to the family farm near Bad Axe. He leased out most of his acreage to a sugar-beet grower, grew enough hops to brew his own beer, and taught algebra on Saturdays to adults at a local community college.

Angelo's attention was diverted when bright floodlights lit the river's edge, illuminating a work crew. *Fixing lead pipes?* It brought back memories of the farmers market, with the conveyor-belt of people passing cases of bottled water, his first meeting with Perry Karas, and listening to Charlie Birnbaum for the first time. *A lifetime ago*, he mused.

Most people expressed their commitment to the group's mission. The two latecomers said they were more skeptical, wary of anything that involved the government. Samuels stated flatly that he wasn't so sure about a government of, by, and for the people. He wasn't convinced an amendment or two could fix that problem. "I agree with the goal of honesty and integrity," he said, "but just remember, 'Trust but verify.'" Angelo found him to be an affable man, but with a high degree of certainty in his opinions.

Cher Richie was a young, pretty woman wearing a floral-patterned hijab. "Yes," she said, "I am a Muslim. I live in Dearborn with others of my faith. What may not be quite so evident is that my parents, my sister, and I are relatively recent U.S. citizens from the once Moorish part of southern Spain. We came here just over ten years ago. I'm a programmer, and some of my comedic colleagues sometimes tease by referring to me as 'our Moor.'" What appealed to her on the list of goals and values was inclusion, diversity and equality of opportunity as well as freedom of religion and separation of church and state. "But the truth is," she said, "I can't find anything on that list I could not commit to. I'm all in."

Angelo listened carefully when Perry Karas said there were three things that mattered to him: his relationship to Henry Ortega and the other kids at Hurley Pediatric, his Greek family heritage, and his strong belief in a true democracy. "If it's okay, let me tell you about an early experience," he said. "I was on the student council in eighth grade. A city councilman named McLaren gave out an award for good citizenship to the middle schools every year. Of course, it was called the McLaren Cup. He would come in to give us his test each year—just one question: 'What is our form of government in this country?' If we answered 'a democracy,' Councilman McLaren would tell us we were wrong. 'We live in a Republic,' he told us. He *wanted* us to give him the wrong answer so he could deliver his little lecture on a representative republic. Then he would go ahead and give us the trophy for another year. Our student council advisor, Mrs. Task, told us exactly what to expect ahead of time and it went exactly as she predicted. I was just an eighth grader, so I didn't argue or anything, but it all seemed so phony to me.

"I had a hockey game that night and, in those days, my Grandmother Achima always took me to lunch on game days. She was my good-luck charm and she also always gave me five dollars for every goal I scored. She picked me up right after the McLaren meeting. I was still kind of confused and, actually, a little pissed about the whole phony business. When I told her about it, she gave me a lesson in Greek history. She told me about democracy in the ancient days of Athens. Ever since then, I have studied—in school and out—about the subject we are here to talk about. The more I learn and the more I see what's going on in this country, the more off track we seem. We need to think about what a real democracy would look like—if we could have one."

Angelo was next and he built on Perry's comments. "It's a good thing we are getting to know each other. I knew Perry Karas as a hockey star. As a pretty good player myself once, I resented him. I could see how good he was—but instead of admiration I felt bitterness. Even anger. He was a white man. I believed that I could have been where he was if I had been a white man." Angelo paused and glanced at Perry. "If we had ever been on the ice together, I would have dropped my gloves.

"I don't feel that way anymore. Perry is not the person I once thought he was. I have had the chance to get to know him better. I've seen him in Flint and what he is doing there.

"I know we are supposed to be talking about ourselves, and here I am talking about Perry Karas. But, believe me, I am also talking about myself. Just weeks ago, I would not have been able to say the things I am saying here. I now see the world in a different way, just as I see Perry in a different way. Before, when I said 'my people,' I was talking about my Native people. Now, *my people* is everyone, including everyone in this room. I know you all bring gifts to this group. I look forward to us unwrapping those gifts.

"I'll be honest. I had to be coaxed to go to Michigan Speaks. I did not, however, have to be coaxed to come here tonight. Some Native people say a time of purification is followed by a time of renewal. I have been in my own purification time, and now I am in my renewal time. I believe we are here to begin the renewal of our state and maybe our country—and I am committed to help."

There was a quiet pause, and then Lana wrapped things up. "Thank you, everyone. Maybe even in our government, we can be 'Pure Michigan.' Tomorrow morning, you begin the serious work. Based on tonight, I know you will do well."

CHAPTER 18

Skeptics in the House

Later that night, when Lana phoned Charlie Birnbaum after the meeting, he could tell she felt enthused. She told him that the members of the group were all she could have hoped for—diverse backgrounds, diverse personalities, and diverse points of view. Some had moved her—Percy Oliver for example, and Angelo RoundSky. Also, the Muslim woman from Spain and Dearborn, Cher Richie—both her outer and inner beauty.

"I bored Joss to death telling her about it. I knew I wouldn't be able to sleep because I'm still processing the evening," she said, "so I thought I would bother you instead.

"No bother, Lana. I'm delighted to hear it. It will actually help *me* sleep *better*. So, thank you for the call. You think they're going to make it, I gather."

"We both know better than to make those kinds of predictions, Charlie, but I think if any group like this can do it, I'll bet on this one. Long way to go, though."

"We'll take it as it comes, then. But I'm glad for the good start."

The following morning, Charlie was not surprised when he got another call from Lana at his office. This one was totally different. He told Rosa, his assistant, to hold his other calls and to shut his office door.

"Legislators Skeptical About Constitution Process" read the headline in the *Free Press*. It was a story of interviews with the two state Representatives that had been at last night's reception and dinner. The two, Thom Jarret, Republican House Minority Leader, and Janice Rison, Democratic Speaker of the House, had returned to Lansing in the same car with the *Free Press* reporter, who had also been at the dinner. The story referred to "Birnbaum's Hail Mary," and the promised "new game." Both Jarrett and Rison, "with a touch of irony in their voices, wished him well" and expressed hope for its success. However, they also shared some degree of skepticism.

"These are all good people," said Jarret, "but they don't know what they're getting themselves into."

Rison, agreed. "They have the highest hopes, the best motives. But they have no experience, no legal backgrounds, no political backgrounds. How can they be expected to accomplish such a complex undertaking?"

The two lawmakers agreed, even with all their experience—even with all the bipartisan goodwill in the world—they would have a hard time accomplishing what Birnbaum's group was expected to accomplish in their spare time.

"Why do we need a so-called new game in the first place?" Jarrett asked. "Other than our new governor, who really thinks we need to change what we have now?"

Rison's answer: "Maybe the voters. Maybe the voters are the ones who want a new game. That's why the governor won. That's why we have a Democratic majority for the first time in years."

Then the two laughed and changed the subject.

Charlie was reading the paper when Rosa transferred Lana's call.

"Those bastards," she said.

Charlie laughed. "Feeling a bit feisty, are we?"

"Not *you*?"

"Both of them have already been in my office to apologize. They said they had no idea it was on the record. Just friendly banter between politicians. They knew the reporter was there, but thought he was just joining in on the banter."

"Those bastards," Lana said again. "The story is out there now. We need public support and political support. This won't help."

"You're right, of course. We need to do a better job. I asked them to join us for a meeting later today. I want you to be there too. We need to reach some understandings. We also need to get our own story out to the press as soon as we can."

"I find it so disappointing after the way our first meeting went."

"I know."

"I was so impressed with these people. Jarett and Rison may be right about some things, but they don't know this group. Strong people; a real potential for leadership. And, they are not a bunch of innocent yokels."

"We need to get that story in the *Free Press* as soon as we can. I'll have our press guy contact them. Maybe even get the same reporter."

"That could be good, or not."

"I'll let them worry about that. But Lana, this is not the end of the world. We'll have much bigger problems than this before we're finished with this. This is just the beginning."

"Of course, you're right, Governor. We're playing a contact sport, as always."

"As Duffy Daugherty said years ago, 'Dancing is a contact sport; football is a collision sport.'"

"Football and politics," Lana said.

"We'll hit them first when we can and hit back hard when we can't. Of course, your amendment is going to change all that."

"So, now it's *mine*? Thanks a lot."

"My ass is on the line even more than yours. Can you be in my office at three to meet these two yahoos?"

CHAPTER 19

The Birth of NITH

Angelo picked up a negative vibe over breakfast. Everyone was talking about Jarrett and Rison. It was their first setback.

Perry kicked off the meeting with a report on his conversation with Lana. "I'm the one she called," he explained, "because she knows me well enough. But, I am no mouthpiece for this group. We should decide how we're going to handle communications. The *Free Press* article is a downer but we can't let that distract us from doing our job. Lana and the governor will handle the politics. We can only control what we can control, and we have plenty on our plate."

There were a few grumbles before Mrs. Edge spoke up. "I've been called a lot of things worse than *naive*, and that's basically what they were calling us."

The youngest member of the group, Lem Tracker, a college senior from Central Michigan University, chimed in. "I don't think they would have said that if they had heard what I heard from the people in this group last night. Like Mr. Karas says, let somebody else worry about that. Let's figure out how we are going to work. Let's get organized."

Angelo knew that Tracker, an African-American under-grad, was a speech student, a prize-winning debater and the current student body president. He also worked as a news reporter for both the campus and local Mt. Pleasant radio stations. The previous evening, he had made a ring-ing attack on the structure and practice of national and state politics. He was no shy youngster.

"Agreed," said Holly Rifkin. She was a widow from the Detroit suburb of Beverly Hills. She had inherited her father's scrap-metal business, which she and her husband had expanded across the state. She had revealed herself as someone not to be messed with. "Everybody agree?" she asked.

"This negative press ..." said Wynn Stewbie, a freelance technology consultant from the exclusive Detroit suburb of Bloomfield Hills. "Let's lose the name. Constitutional Council? That sounds like another stuffy bureaucratic institution. If we are going to change a bureaucracy, let's start with ourselves."

"I hated that name since it was first announced," said Nick Lahti from the Upper Peninsula town of Hough-ton. "Can't say I have a better suggestion though."

Angelo saw Tom Samuels pitch forward in his chair, knocking his West Point ring on the table. "Around *my* house, I've just been referring to us as the 'Names in the Hat Group.' My wife told me it's too long, so I shortened it to NITH—N-I-T-H." He looked down and snorted a nervous laugh. "She looked it up to see if it was already used or if it meant something else bad. She found a defi-nition of *Nith* online in the Urban Dictionary. It means 'a term of respect usually given to the bond between great friends. Also used to describe an individual with strong leadership qualities.' That's good enough for me, and I don't think we should waste any more time with it." He looked up, gave his ring another rap, and said, "What do you think?"

NITH it was from then on.

Perry said, "What's next? Do we elect officers? I don't think we need a complicated structure, but we do need someone for people like Lana to contact to find out what's going on."

"We need somebody who's clearly in charge," said Samuels. "A clear chain of command is important."

"Spoken like a true army officer," laughed Wayne Keith.

"Well, as the guy in charge in your high school, don't you agree with me?" asked the retired colonel.

Keith said, "I was just having some fun with you. But how formal should a chain of command be in this small group? There's twenty-five of us. We only have one task in front of us. I'm not sure we need a full slate of officers."

"We may need a few special roles—things like a liaison person for outside contacts and so forth," said Martha Smith. "We can still keep it pretty simple."

"Wynn, you look like you've got something on your mind, the way you're running your hand through your hair like it's on fire," said Perry.

"This whole discussion is unbelievable," laughed Stewbie. "Hierarchies and bureaucratic forms of governance are what got us where we are now. With all due respect, Colonel, they may have served their purpose where you came from, but things have changed. Maybe the military still needs it, I don't know. I know so-called leaderless or semi-autonomous groups have been successfully tried for years, even in the Marines. We're in the age of networks.

Like I said, I'm a Peer Progressive politically; so this discussion this early in our work together is just driving me up a wall. People I work with would be going batshit crazy."

The colonel laughed and smiled affably at Stewbie. "With all due respect, I had no idea what you were talking about last night with that Peer Progressive stuff; and I still don't. All I know is that when I hear the word *progressive*, I hear *liberal*. I know all there is to know about liberals. For one thing, liberals don't believe there is such a thing as evil." He chuckled at his own comment.

Angelo could see that behind his friendly smile, Samuels was dead serious. The tone of the meeting had shifted slightly from last night's amicable start. People were being polite but there were clenched fists under the table.

Stewbie's response to Samuels was also polite, with an edge. "You know what, Thomas …"

"Tom is fine."

"You may not believe this, Tom, but I agree with you. *Progressive* connotes *liberal* or *left* and that just gets in the way of the whole set of concepts I'm talking about. I think it's fair of me to guess that you believe in neoliberalism, another confusing term for a whole other socio-economic-political framework which has dominated our politics at least since the end of the Eisenhower administration."

"You calling me a liberal?" Samuels laughed.

"Heaven forbid. Just pointing out how we get confused by labels. As for your understanding of what Peer Progressives really stand for, I'll try to clear that up as we go along. For now, all I want to say is that Peer Progressives are neither liberal nor conservative. We don't think in those terms. We can talk about all that another time though. Right now, we're trying to get organized. All I'm suggesting is that we think in terms of a peer network instead of a pyramidal chain of command."

"Here we go again," laughed Samuels.

"Perry, what about you?" It was Carl Boyd, a production worker at Ford's Wyandotte plant, and a big Wings fan. "You were an assistant captain for the Red Wings, right? How did that work?"

"There's always a designated leader on the ice, a captain or an assistant. He's the only one who can contact or be contacted by an official during the course of play. Informally, on the ice, your coach and your teammates rely on that player's leadership, but other players lead when they need to. It works pretty well."

"Okay, how about that then?" Boyd said. "We just have a couple captains for when we need them. Seems simple enough."

Angelo finally spoke. "The Grand Traverse Band has what I call a 'big, old, white man's constitution.' Back when the federal government made us get rid of our clan system and forced us into a representative form of government and direct elections of our chiefs. Our constitution is as full of *whereas* and *heretofore* as any fat, legal document—but the fact is, many of our Algonkian ancestor tribes from earlier times were organized in the way we are now talking. Some of our people are trying to return to our old ways of governing. Back then, chiefs were sort of like Perry's ice captains. Most of the time, they were just temporary. There might be a battle chief, for instance, but once the battle was over, he went right back to being just another member of the tribe. In fact," Angelo continued, smiling, "they made him go through a cleansing rite to get all that chief stuff out of him."

"Glad I didn't have to do that," Perry joked.

"Isn't that fascinating?" said Susan Kerns, her dark eyes and smile revealing her delight. "As a new state legislator and a person with a big interest in history, I find all of this very interesting. Any other examples of special chiefs?"

"If you don't mind, Angelo, can you speak a little louder?" asked Samuels. "Last night I found it a hard to hear you, and, like Susan here, I'm interested in what you are telling us about the Algonkians. Or is it Algonquins?"

"Algonkians, and I'll try to talk a little louder but first I have to explain. Growing up, I didn't have a lot of positive role models. Maybe a tribal elder or two. My hockey coaches were all screamers who liked to humiliate their players. When I got older, I came to admire two men a lot for what they stood for—Nelson Mandela and a football coach, Tony Dungy. Both were men of integrity. They showed great dignity, even when they were in tough situations. I noticed they always spoke quietly and calmly. As a hockey player who loved to fight, that was not my style, but I wanted to be like them. So, I will try to talk a little louder, but you may also just have to listen a little harder if you want to hear me."

"Okay," said Susan Kerns, "I'm listening harder. Now, what about those chiefs?"

"These tribes weren't much for power or authority. Like me, they didn't like to take orders. They considered themselves moral people. They didn't need others telling them how to act. That was demeaning. They saw power as a dangerous thing. That's why most special leadership jobs were temporary. One elder, because of the lineage in his clan, did act as more permanent village chief, but about all he could do was call a meeting. He was mainly thought of as a peace chief. He helped settle arguments—like a counselor. And there was a ceremony leader, a true elder who knew all the rites, but had no power except to be the memory for the tribal rituals—and only when they needed them."

Samuels laughed. "No chain of command? No wonder they lost all the time."

The joke fell flat and irritated Angelo. Nevertheless, he managed to keep his quiet voice and said, "When the Nazis lost, didn't they have a clear leader and chain of command? And the Japanese? And the Confederate army? And, how about us Americans in Vietnam and Afghanistan?"

Quick to change the subject, Harold "Skip" Marshall, a black fireman from Detroit, said, "Let's just have a captain or whatever you want to call it when a need comes up. Permanent or temporary, I don't care. And maybe that depends on the situation."

Angelo was relieved to get back on topic.

"So far, a contact person for people outside our group to get in touch with," said Susan Kerns.

"Maybe that's enough for now," said Marshall. "We can figure out the rest as we go."

"Do we need a moderator for our meetings? Just asking," said Lauren Bommarito, a young nurse from Grand Rapids.

"Somebody needs to be in charge," said Samuels.

"Let's just play that by ear," said Stewbie. "Start without one and see what happens."

Marshall said, "I'm good with that."

They voted. All hands went up except Samuels and Edges.

"Done," said Marshall. "Now, who's our liaison captain then?"

"Perry, you've been the one so far," said Richard Berger, the swarthy Grosse Pointe insurance-company manager. Like some of the others, he was clearly becoming impatient. Although he was speaking up for the first time, Angelo remembered him from last night as being fairly aggressive.

"I'll do it for now," Perry said. "That way we can get onto other things. But I like Angelo's idea of temporary chiefs. I'll be glad to hand this off anytime in the future."

"Okay then," Berger said. "Our name is NITH and Perry's our temporary liaison chief. Now, can we get down to business? What are we really here for?"

"If I can suggest," said Cher Richie, "before we get to that question, we should talk about how we are going to involve other people. Lana and Governor Birnbaum have both emphasized that we are not to do all this in private. They want broad participation. I propose we have a presence on Facebook and Twitter, as well as a blog or website of our own."

"I'd be glad to set that up," said Stewbie.

"Let me know if I can help," said Richie.

"And I'll be glad to start a blog," said Percy Oliver.

The simple question of what they were there for would take time to resolve. The question would come back again and again throughout the group's life. Weaving in and out of the obvious answer—to draft an amendment or amendments to the state constitution—were discussions about the meanings of democracy, hierarchy, networks, liberal, conservative, left vs. right, civility, and issues such as national politics, building a wall, climate change, abortion rights, deadlines, and frustrations. What the hell is the governor talking about when he says we need a new game?

They took a break midmorning. Members, like Angelo, got on their phones or talked in small groups. Some took a short stroll along the Flint River. Some expressed concern about how the morning had gone and wondered if they were going to be up to the task.

"Okay, look," said Samuels, when they reconvened. "We're not making much progress here. Everyone agree?"

He waited. Silence.

"I'll take that to mean consent. Before we break for lunch, can we just agree that a moderator might help? No big chain of command, just a simple moderator? I nominate our young star, Lem Tracker. Can we have a show of hands?" All hands went up, some more slowly than others.

At first, Tracker seemed surprised, but then he smiled broadly. "I'll do the best I can. Thank you," he said.

Angelo got a kick out the young man's confidence. It was clear Lem thought his best would be plenty good enough.

"Good, then," said Samuels. "I move we all go have lunch."

"Just one more thing," said Tracker. "We're not getting too far as this whole group. I think maybe we should break up into subgroups this afternoon."

This also turned out to be more than a simple decision. Before Tracker pushed the group to resolution, there was substantial disagreement—with some arguing that they needed to stick together as one team, and others arguing they would work more efficiently in smaller groups. When Tracker asked for a show of hands, it was decided by a close vote to try subgroups for the afternoon and to meet as a whole just before quitting time to hear reports. Groups were set up and topics assigned.

Angelo sat at a lunch table with Perry, Wynn Stewbie, Susan Kerns, and Marta Orosco. He was a little surprised when Stewbie started the conversation with, "Did you all see that power move?"

Kerns also looked surprised and asked what he meant by his question.

Stewbie answered, "Samuels. I'm talking about his nomination of Lem for moderator."

"What was wrong with that?" asked Kerns. "I thought it was nice to ask our youngest member, and a minority at that."

"So, you're going into a career in politics?" Stewbie asked her.

"Now who's being condescending?" she shot back.

"Sorry, you're absolutely right. Pretty hypocritical, I'll grant you. But I've seen it so many times in workshops I've done. Nobody usually wants to volunteer for those jobs, so a powerful member of the group—usually a guy, I confess—quickly nominates one of the least powerful, like a woman, say, or the youngest or the one African American in the group. In this case, Samuels got a two for one."

Kerns replied, "I think you're just being cynical."

Orosco, who had not said anything all morning, agreed. "I think it was nice."

Perry finally spoke up. "Well, I don't know who's right, but if Samuels thinks he got a pushover, he's got another think coming."

Angelo said, "Me too. That kid is smart and sure of himself."

Susan Kerns turned back to Stewbie and said with a smile, "Are you worried about your own influence in the group, Wynn?"

Stewbie returned her smile with a sheepish but good-natured grin. "You nailed me, Susan. Didn't think of that, but maybe I am. I wish Lem all the best in the world, though. You guys are right. He's certainly not a shrinking violet."

CHAPTER 20

Subject to Dispute

When Angelo's subgroup met that afternoon to discuss government structure, Samuels started things off with a friendly question followed by his usual chuckle. "Are we going for a consensus? If so, I think we're here for the duration.

Stewbie said, "Look, I think we should just share our thoughts about structure for a while and see if that gets us anywhere. If we can't agree, we just report back that we agree to disagree and come back to it later."

"Shoot," said Samuels.

"I ran a large company," said Edges. "With over four hundred bookstores, for several years, and very successfully. Then the world of book sellers nosedived almost everywhere. I tried to treat all my employees well, at all levels, but it was no democracy. There was no question of who was in charge."

"Ditto for the military," said Samuels. "But I also worked for a private company after I retired. I agree with Maddy. People-oriented, yes. Democracy, no."

Karas interjected. "But we're not talking about running a business here."

"That is exactly the problem," said Edges.

"I don't believe a government can or should be run like a business," said Karas. "It's an entirely different animal. Governor Stenhouse—or should I say, ex-governor—showed us that. You can't just go into a city in trouble, shove their duly elected officials aside, and put a business executive in charge. That should be against the law. Arbitrarily seizing power from democratically elected officials might even be unconstitutional. Look at the mess it got us in Flint. Look at Henry Ortega, if you want a sad for instance. We have a businessman in the White House right now. You want to talk about a mess."

"Not sure we want to get into all that here," said Samuels. "Let's agree to stick to Michigan, okay? You said you learned way back that the US constitution calls for a republic, right? Are you telling me they were wrong? Are you telling me that we're smarter than James Madison and Alexander Hamilton?"

"I thought we were sticking to Michigan," reminded Angelo.

Karas said, "I'd like to answer that. I have all the respect in the world for our founders. I think they showed great courage and risked their lives and fortunes on a grand experiment. They are heroes to me and most Americans. I'm just a hockey player. I never ran a company. But I have been serious about politics since the eighth grade. My only year at U of M, I studied poly sci. My beliefs run deep. The founders were *people* too. They lived in a different time. They set up a whole structure for white, landed males, just like themselves. There weren't nearly as *many* people or as large an area to consider—just thirteen states, all in the east—and even with that, they were much more spread out and less educated. Jefferson is one of my heroes, despite his wobbly slavery behavior. He emphasized things like education and a free press as basic necessities for a democracy. What would he think about all the information available to us today?"

"Maybe too *much* information," answered Edges.

"Funny thing for a book person to say," said RoundSky.

"And not all valid information either," said Edges. "We've certainly been learning that. All that fake news."

"Everybody knows I come from Greek roots," said Karas.

"The Greek freak," said Samuels.

"Yeah," said Karas. "I don't like that very much but there it is. If you want to examine the history of democracy, let's go all the way back, way before 1776, to ancient Greece. I am proud to say that the word *democracy*—which means 'rule by the people'—comes from the Greek. One guy, Solon, *their* founding father, laid out the framework for governing the city state of Athens. Things changed by the time of Pericles and the so-called Golden Age and their government evolved with the changing times. They picked their governing bodies by lot, just like we do with our juries now. Think about the way *we* got here, getting our names drawn out of a hat. Same thing. Only free, male landowners, of course. Pretty much the way we started in this country. Thankfully, our system has evolved some, at least on that score."

"Madison called it 'rule by the mob,'" said Samuels. "I think he was probably right."

"Look up Pericles's funeral oration," suggested Karas.

"But it eventually collapsed, right?" asked Edges.

Karas answered. "Yeah. Like a lot of things ... I'm sorry, Madeline. That was thoughtless of me to say it like that.

I meant no system lasts forever. Nor should it. That's why we're here."

"If their lottery idea was so great," said Samuels, "why didn't other countries try it?"

"They *did*," said Karas. "It was used successfully in Venice and other Italian city states. Recently it was used in Iceland and British Columbia in the form of citizen assemblies. Pretty much the way we did with Speaks and NITH."

"Ridiculous," said Edges. "We're never going to pick our officials names out of a hat. Think of the unqualified people we could end up with."

Karas chuckled. "Like we have now, you mean? Unqualified? Corrupt? Could drawing names be any worse? I'm not trying to make a joke of this. Back up a minute. I'm not here to sell sortition, which is actually what government by lot is called. I'm just saying, if you want to go back in history to make your case, back to Madison and Hamilton and Jefferson—all radicals for their time—you can go back even further to make an even more radical case."

"You guys all sound like liberals," said Samuels. "I told you what I think of liberals."

"I don't think of myself as a liberal *or* as a conservative," corrected Stewbie. "Those labels don't serve us well today; if they ever did. Same with Democrat and Republican. The labels hurt more than they help."

"Sounds like something a liberal would say," said Samuels.

"Believe it or not," said Stewbie, "on some things I'm a libertarian. In many areas, the marketplace is democracy at work. People making daily decisions on their own on what they need or want. But I don't think the marketplace works for everything. It can't solve all of society's problems. So, on some things I believe we need the public sector. And sometimes we don't need either one. We just need people working together in open, collaborative networks."

"I don't know what that means," said Samuels. "Some middle-of-the-road, wishy-washy mash up."

"No," said Stewbie. "That still keeps us stuck in those old models, those old divisive frameworks, just trying to find a compromise between the two. What I *am* pushing—and I guess it's fair to call it pushing—is that we forget those old labels and go back to the drawing board. I'm talking about a whole new philosophy. Yes to markets but no libertarian panacea for everything. Yes to a role for the public sector but no to the old leftist notion of state-centralized panaceas. I'm talking about things like peer-to-peer networks."

Samuels couldn't let it rest. "More progressive mumbo jumbo?"

Stewbie smiled. "I do believe in making progress, don't you, Tom?"

"Like we're doing now?" said Edges.

"Touché," said Karas. "Angelo? What's on your mind?"

"History," answered RoundSky. "I mentioned the history of some the Algonkian tribes this morning. I am Anishinaabe. The Algonkians are *my* ancestors. They didn't believe in a pyramid structure either. Where most white people looked up to heaven for an all-powerful god, Natives believe our spirits are all around us, in the directions of the four winds. More horizontal. Gods at the edges of the universe instead of up there somewhere. And the spirits were not all-powerful. They were pretty much on the same level as humans. And that's also how these tribes governed themselves—horizontally. As I said this morning, they didn't hand power to anyone on a permanent basis."

"Another crazy idea," said Edges.

"Wait a minute, Maddy," said Samuels. "I am finding all this quite fascinating."

"Don't patronize me," warned RoundSky.

"Not at all. I would like to understand your culture better," said Samuels.

"For him, it's exotic," said Edges.

"I'm not here as an exotic. And I'm not here to represent Natives or anyone else. I'm here as myself, and I'm trying, like all of you are, to get down to what we can agree is a way out of the political mess we are in as a state and a country. *My* state and *my* country."

"This is good," said Karas. "We have two historical precedents—the Athenians and the Algonkians—aligning with each other *and* with an innovative new model that Wynn is proposing. That's pretty thought-provoking for me."

"Exotic and weird, if you ask me," said Edges.

"That's true of any paradigm different from the one we are used to," said Stewbie. "I'm happy to learn from both of these historical precedents. They resonate with a paradigm that I have been exploring. Let's be clear, though. They are not the same. Despite their similarities, each is a unique system that fits a unique culture at a unique time in the history of that culture."

"What I have been hearing Perry say is that the US constitution created a new and different system that fit that culture at that time," said RoundSky. "A white man's culture—I have to add—that was a reaction to another older, white man's culture. A break from the past and a brave one, a painful one for many people to swallow. It has served well for many years. But times are different now. And then I hear Wynn telling us we may need to be brave and break from the past once again."

"You are obviously smart guys," Samuels said. "But I have to say, I think you're all nuts."

"Amen," agreed Edges.

"The Greek system eventually failed, as did the system in Venice and other places," said Samuels. "Those proposals in British Columbia and Iceland also got shot down in the end. And, Angelo, those tribes didn't do so well either, did they? Wynn, your stuff is interesting, but at this point, all it adds up to is an intellectual exercise."

"Nations and empires in the past have disappeared for all kinds of reasons," said Stewbie. "Just as businesses have, I might add. Countries with kings, emperors, or pharaohs up top running things. Or dictators. The British Empire went from royal rulers to a parliamentary system before it faded from the world scene. And your military chain of command, Thomas? The Roman Legions, the Spanish Armada, Napoleon's armies, and on and on. Did they all get their butts beat because they had a clear chain of command or were there other reasons?

"As for peer networks, I could easily bore you with all kinds of real-world success stories from old times right up to the present day. The question is, what do we do now? We're almost out of time for the afternoon. We are supposed to report back to the others in about fifteen minutes."

"All we can tell them is that we have agreed to disagree," Karas said. "We will need more time to work through it."

"Or not," Edges said.

"Why don't we do what the US Supreme Court does?"

Karas suggested. "Someone will write a majority opinion and someone else will write the minority opinion. I think we all know where we stand right now."

"And the majority opinion will stand as a final decision, like it does with the court?" asked Edges. "I'm not buying that."

"No. I don't mean that," said Karas. "I think the total NITH process is a long way from any final decisions. We don't have to settle anything yet. Let's lay out our opinions as they stand now. The big group can dig into them if they want or send us back for more or get some other people to work on it."

"I can go with that," said Samuels. "Maddy, you're a good writer. Why don't you write up our minority opinion?"

"Oops, he did it again," said Stewbie.

Angelo and Perry smile at each other and Wynn.

"Who's going to write ours?" asked RoundSky.

"Let's all three of us try to do it together after dinner," suggested Perry.

CHAPTER 21

All in a Night's Work

People seemed pleased with the overall progress of the day. The larger group had started work on a Bill of Responsibilities that reflected the values expressed at the Michigan Speaks conference in January. "It's only our first day," moderator Tracker said. "We don't have to settle everything yet. I think we had a good day, everybody. Let's have a nice dinner and a relaxing evening; then we'll get back at it in the morning."

Angelo skipped the happy hour to stroll along the riverside before calling Lexi He was struck by the contrast between the clear waters surrounding his upstate home and the murky Flint River. One was life, he thought, the other was death. When he reached Lexi he scarcely got started on the day's ups and downs when she interrupted. "Angelo, just be quiet a minute. I want to hear all about it but I have to tell you something important first."

"What is it? Is everything okay, I hope?"

"Even better. I'm pregnant. We're going to have a baby."

She began to describe her discovery, her feelings—but Angelo could hardly follow anything she was saying. He no longer cared about his own day. He managed to spit out a few questions that made almost no sense. He couldn't focus on her answers. She was telling him she had been hoping it would happen ever since his return from North Manitou. She said that it had been awhile since her last period, that she had done the home test, and that she had seen her doctor that day, who confirmed it. "I didn't want to tell you until I knew for sure," she said. "But, you're going to be a daddy. How about that?"

"Lex, I can't believe it. Nothing could make me happier. We need to get married, Lexi. I want to be your husband when our baby is born."

"Me too. That's what I want. We can do it, Ang. We'll make that happen real soon. Now, tell me about your day."

"To hell with that. Your day surpasses mine big time. I'll tell you more about it when I calm down. Now, I'm going to go celebrate with a drink, if I haven't already missed all of the happy hour. I love you, babe. I can't tell you how much."

"I love you too, Daddy. Have a drink for me. I won't be having any for a while."

Through the haze of his thoughts, Angelo ordered a drink and watched his fellow group members mingle. When others tried to engage him in conversation, he nodded and smiled but heard little of what they said. Throughout dinner, he mindlessly picked at his food. When his subgroup met to work on the so-called "majority report" in Perry's room, he was still pretty much blanked out. He decided he had to say something. He had to explain his distraction. When he shared his news, they did everything but dance around the room with him.

"Let's all just blow it off and go celebrate," said Wynn.

"Please, no, guys," urged Angelo. "I don't want to be

responsible for that. We need to have something ready for tomorrow. I just don't know how much help I can be."

"Look," said Perry, "why don't you take the rest of the night off? Wynn and I can put something together for the morning."

"I know you can," Angelo said, "and I would trust what you came up with. But I don't want to just go back to my room, either. I would just drive myself crazy. How about I just stay here, you two discuss, and I'll try to listen. If I think of anything to add, I'll stick it in, but don't count on it."

"Right," Wynn said.

Angelo stretched out on the one unused queen bed in Perry's room. He pulled a pillow out from the comforter and lay his head on it. The other two laughed at him and got started.

"So," said Perry, "we talked about everything from ancient Greece to the Algonkian tribes. Wynn, you expanded on your peer networks idea. They all seem to point in a common direction."

"That direction," said Wynn, "is horizontal not vertical, am I right?"

"I liked Angelo's description of the gods or spirits at the edges of the universe instead of above somewhere. We should use that."

From the bed, Angelo said, "Not just the edges, all around us. The realms are all around us."

"He *talks*," teased Wynn. "That's even better than the horizontal idea. I like that a lot. The kinds of networks I have in mind go in all different directions. There is no central point or funnel that everything has to pass through." He cited theories, research, and examples from authorities with names like Legrand and Hayek and Baran. Perry nodded as he listened, but said he was only able to grasp about half of it. Angelo barely paid attention, only picking up a thread here and there.

There was a knock on the door. Perry opened it to see Cher Richie. It would be unusual for a Muslim woman to be in a room with three men at night, but then Cher was an unusually independent woman.

"Sorry, guys," she said. "I don't want to get in the way but I'm very interested in what you're doing. I was with the so-called Inclusion group this afternoon, for obvious reasons, but I think what you guys are working on affects everything else so much I wanted to be in on this one too. I have been interested in networks and the P2P people for a while now. I would love to learn more."

"P2P people?" Angelo said. "Sounds like 'The Walking Dead.'"

"Peer to peer," said Wynn. "Go to sleep."

It was the first Cher had noticed Angelo on the far bed.

"He's had some exciting news from home," Wynn said to Cher. "He's been useless ever since."

Cher smiled and shrugged.

"We're sworn to secrecy," said Perry.

"Go ahead and tell her," Angelo called. "What the hell?"

Wynn and Perry filled her in and she was as excited as they had been at the news.

"But that's all," he said. "Nobody else."

"My lips are sealed," said Cher.

"Enough. Get back to work," Angelo said.

Wynn briefly summed up their ideas. Cher chimed in with questions and comments. They set to work on the wording of a draft to present in the morning. Angelo pretty much absented himself from the process.

When the three agreed on the basics, Perry suggested Wynn smooth it out for the presentation. "You're the wordsmith," he said. "And you should give enough information about the peer-network idea so people can really get it."

Wynn interrupted. "You need to do it, Perry. Nobody wants to hear a lecture from me. You have more credibility than anybody in that whole room."

"I totally agree," said Cher.

After a short protest, Perry gave in but asked Cher if she would work with him. "I would appreciate your input."

"You got it," she said.

They looked to Angelo to get his blessing, but the father to be could only nod. They decided to leave him alone. She and Perry finished their work in the early-morning hours when she left to get some sleep of her own.

Lying on his own bed, Perry attempted to tweak things a while longer, before beginning to snore. Angelo jumped at the sound of the snoring and, once oriented, left to go to his own room.

CHAPTER 22

Imagine

Perry, Wynn, Cher, and Angelo checked in with each other at breakfast to review Perry and Cher's work on their majority report. Before they got down to business, they asked Angelo how his night went.

"Fine, until my buddy Perry here started snoring," he said. "I don't know if I slept a wink after I got back to my room. I hope I can be a little more help today."

Just as they looked Perry's way for a discussion of his night's activity, his cell rang out with the Red Wing fight song. "I better take it. It's Lana," he said, reading the caller ID. "Hi, I'm having breakfast with Angelo and Wynn and Cher. Cher and I are making a presentation to the entire group this morning. I'll put you on speaker, if you don't mind."

"How's it going?" Lana said. She was in higher spirits than might have been expected after the bad press of yesterday.

Angelo answered. "We didn't all sit around a campfire and smoke a peace pipe. Nobody held hands and sang "Kumbaya," but we ended up in a pretty good place."

"A *very* good place for Angelo," Perry said. "Did you hear his news?"

"No. What's up?" said Lana.

"He found out last night that he's going to be a father," said Perry.

"What wonderful news, Angelo! Is this your first? I think I met your wife."

"Lexi, and technically she's not my wife—yet. Soon will be, though. But can we not spread this around too much? I'm not sure Lexi even wanted me to tell anybody yet. I was just in such a crazy place last night, I had to tell somebody."

Lana said, "Your secret is safe with me. But that's great news. Now, I have some news for all of you. You read the *Free Press* yesterday morning, about the two state House members and their comments about the group. Well, a couple things. We got that partially straightened out with them, yesterday afternoon, in Governor Birnbaum's office."

"I'll bet that was some meeting," said Wynn.

"Actually, not so bad. All very congenial—even a little kumbaya, as a matter of fact. We promised to keep them in the loop and even seek out their input. They promised not to block things or gossip to reporters anymore. They're both politicians, so we'll just have to wait and see how that goes. Another thing. You remember Jimmy Owens wrote some nice things after Michigan Speaks. He's ready to write another column on our progress. Not a puff piece. He wants to see how things are going, maybe write something for this Sunday's paper. Your meeting winds up at lunch today; he would like to meet some people there, right after it concludes, to get their take on things. I thought the new 'production line' might give him the scoop."

"New production line?" asked Wynn.

"Perry, Angelo, and me," said Lana. "Back in the day, with the Red Wings, they had Howe, Lindsay, and Abel. They were called the 'Production Line.' Perry, Angelo, and I have a hockey connection. I thought it might be fun if I played center to those two snipers, feed them the puck, so they can score."

Cher said, "I'm getting lost in the hockey analogies. I'm not really a hockey fan or much of a sports fan in general, actually. But, if you mean you want Jimmy Owens to interview some people, you should at least include Lem Tracker. He's our moderator and he's doing a good job."

"Absolutely," said Perry.

"Got it," said Lana. "Glad you gave the young man a job."

"We'll let everybody know Owen is coming," Perry said. "By the way, Lana, we are not the Constitutional Council anymore. We're NITH, short for Names in the Hat. We came up with that when we were in the kumbaya stage."

"That's even better," said Lana. "We can use that when we talk with Owens. I hope you guys know that kumbaya is actually a hymn pleading for God's help."

"We could use some," said Angelo.

"See you at lunch," Lana said.

"Now," said Wynn, addressing Perry and Cher, "we're running out of time here. What have you two planned for our report?"

Perry smiled. "I hope you still want to call it 'ours' after it's over. Despite Angelo's report on my snoring, I didn't get much sleep last night. Cher and I dug through our notes and pulled something together. Unfortunately, there's no time to walk you through it and get your feedback. It looks like we're just going to have to wing it."

"You'll do a great job," Wynn said.

"Please chip in when you feel like it. We don't want to give the impression that this is all coming from me."

"I'm in," said Wynn. He looked toward Angelo and said, "Dad?"

"Just worry about yourself," Angelo grumbled good-naturedly.

While Perry and Cher set up the projector and computer, Lem Tracker told the group that he had been reading Kurt Vonnegut in his American Lit class. "Maybe we're going about this all wrong," he said. "In his novel *Cat's Cradle,* a guy named Bokonon invents a new religion—something like what we are trying to do here." Tracker picked up a paperback and read:

> *"Let us start our Republic with a chain of drug stores, a chain of grocery stores, a chain of gas chambers, and a national game. After that we can write our constitution."*

When the laughter died down, Perry filled the group in on Lana's phone call. They were happy to have the opportunity to correct the impressions of the two House leaders. They designated one person from each subgroup to talk with Jimmy Owens after lunch. Edges would represent the minority report of the Structure group. Angelo recognized the risk in that but hoped it would add to the authenticity of the interview. They weren't telling only the rosy side of the story. Besides, opinions might have changed by the end of the day.

Tracker then asked Perry to give his presentation. Perry stood as Cher punched up the first slide from the computer.

We the People, All the People

Music began to fill the room. It was John Lennon singing his and Yoko Ono's words to the song "Imagine." The final lyrics appeared on the next slide:

> *You may say I'm a dreamer*
> *But I'm not the only one*
> *I hope someday you'll join us*
> *And the world will be as one.*

Wynn and Angelo made eye contact and exchanged small smiles as Perry spoke. "Some have already accused this group of being dreamers, including Mrs. Edges and Mr. Samuels. We accept that. But so is our sponsor, Governor Birnbaum. He has asked us not to settle for small change.

"I do have a dream. But I think I'm a practical dreamer. Most of what we propose has been, or is now, in actual practice somewhere. But, like the song says, to accomplish our mission, we need to do the hardest thing of all: We need to think differently. Right, Wynn? We need to imagine. That requires us all to be dreamers. Join us in imagining a different political world than the one we live in now."

A series of slides followed, while Perry commented:

> *Imagine a state government you can TRUST. A government with complete transparency, in which all the people are connected interactively with each other and to their government.*

"Remember the report handed out at Michigan Speaks? It was a report of a recent opinion survey of Michigan residents titled "Fractured Trust." Lack of trust in our state government is the number one concern for the people in Michigan. One of the citizens in the study said, 'It's very difficult to have trust in a government that has, over a long period of time, declined to respond to its citizens.'

"The form of government we are advocating for this morning hits at the heart of this problem. We have the technology to make government open, transparent, and interactive. We are not talking about 'internet utopia,' though the internet does give us tools to turn this dream into a reality if we have the imagination and the political will to do it."

Tom Samuels interrupted. "Excuse me just a minute. I don't mean to put a wrench into this presentation, but you guys are putting a lot of faith in the internet. I mean, how's that working out lately? Hackers stealing all our personal information. Identity theft. Maybe even the Russians interfering with the last Presidential election. Why should we let ourselves in for even more trouble with what you are proposing?"

Angelo got a kick out of Perry's stumped expression. "I think I better let Cher answer that," Perry said. "She and Wynn are my technology gurus."

Cher stood, smiled, and dove in. "Tom is absolutely right. Like we said, the internet is not the utopian dream some people once thought it was. The last few years have exposed some major flaws. We went from an open, decentralized internet to companies like Facebook, Twitter, and Google with centralized hierarchical systems and closed boundaries—just the opposite of what we are proposing for our government. These hierarchies are an added layer on top of the original internet architecture. I'm glad to say that the whole Bitcoin phenomenon may be changing that."

"Oh, god," Samuels interjected, "surely you're not going to try to sell us on that pyramid scheme."

Cher laughed and replied, "I gather you are not among those who are getting rich on Bitcoin. No, that is not what I am saying. What I mean is that Bitcoin has introduced a new layer of internet architecture called "blockchain," which has many other applications. It is a new level of networking that is itself decentralized, with no central authority. It operates strictly on the peer-to-peer basis that Wynn has been advocating. And with complete transparency. Unlike what we have now, where Facebook, for instance, owns your personal information and can basically do whatever it wants with it. What we propose is using an application that only you can access and a network that is so widely distributed no hacker can get into your information. This technology is just now taking hold, and we expect a great many new applications in the near future, including, I'm glad to say, applications for better governance."

Maddy Edges snapped, "Just more voodoo, if you ask me."

Lem Tracker sighed and intervened. "Maddy and Tom, you'll have your chance. Let's listen to the rest of their report."

Cher thanked Lem and put up the next slide.

Imagine a state government in which all the people are able to be engaged in governance deliberations and deci-

sions at any and all times at their choice, rather than just at election time.

"Yesterday this group we call NITH stated that we are committed to the idea, the ideal, of a government of the people, for the people, and by the people. Make no mistake, we do not have that now. Some of us vote every two or four years. Many don't even do that. That's the extent of our governing as the people. And even that is arguably more symbolic than real. We call it our choice but we choose between a duopoly of the two major parties, mostly bought and paid for by the persuasion industry—PACs and SUPERPACs, special-interest groups, and lobbyists of all stripes. Voting districts are gerrymandered to protect one party from defeat by the other party. At election time we often feel we are forced to choose the lesser of two evils. Ever heard that before at election time? Ever said it yourself? I certainly have. We complain—but it feels like complaining about the weather. 'It's just the way it is,' we say.

"That, my fellow NITHs, is what we now call government of, by and for the people. We cast our vote, such as it is, and from that point on turn things over to a centralized hierarchy of political elites whose primary motivation is to get reelected by making the other guys look bad. The rest of their time is spent raising more cash for that same reason."

Imagine a state government that looks less like a pyramid/more like a circle; less vertical/more horizontal; less centralized/more peer-to-peer networks.

"This is not a New Age dream," Perry continued. "It has been a part of America's culture since the beginning of our country. Cher?"

From her seat by the computer, Cher said, "As a relatively new and proud American citizen, I've tried hard to learn all I could about this country, a little like Alexis de Tocqueville did as an outsider looking in. Way back in 1840 he wrote: 'Americans group together to hold fêtes, found seminaries, build inns, construct churches, distribute books, dispatch missionaries to the antipodes. They establish hospitals, prisons, schools by the same method. Finally, if they wish to highlight a truth or develop an opinion by the encouragement of a great example, they form an association.' *But,* he also said, 'It often happens that, in democratic countries, a large number of men who want or need to form an association cannot do so because they fail to see or find each other. ... Then a newspaper appears to publish the opinion or idea which had occurred simultaneously but separately to each of them. ... The newspaper has brought them together and continues to be necessary to keep them together.'

"As Perry said, with the internet, today we don't have to wait for a newspaper to print a story. We have mass media, email, websites, blogs, live streaming, and a host of social media sites to bring people together into what de Tocqueville called 'associations.' Wynn uses the term 'peer-to-peer networks.' These associations have existed as long as there have been people. But today, the internet provides us with a social architecture that makes these associations easier to create."

Imagine a government in which the conservatives' goal

of freedom and the liberals' goal of equality are mutually realized.

Imagine a state government without political parties, with less partisan divisiveness, less concern with liberal vs. conservative, less left vs. right, more concern with finding solutions that work for the people.

Cher said, "We use de Tocqueville again because we want you to know that our dreams here are grounded in principle dating all the way back to the founding of America. He said: 'There are many men of principle in both parties in America, but there is no party of principle.'"

"Sound familiar?" Perry said. "This was written in 1835. What we are proposing, is not left-wing or right-wing, not liberal or conservative. Big government versus the marketplace is just another false dichotomy we have created for ourselves, like Republican and Democrat. We unequivocally reject these old labels, these old dichotomies. Nor, as Wynn has explained, are we talking about a squishy place in the middle.

"The kind of bottom-up, two-way, non hierarchical structure we envision is the opposite of the box we are in, with our current thinking about government. We have to think outside that box. While we learn from the past, we take responsibility to avoid the irrational clinging to ideology that afflicted liberalism in the 1970s and 80s and conservatism today. Although the word *paradigm* has been overused and may have lost some of its meaning, what we are talking to you about this morning deserves being called a *new paradigm.*"

Imagine a state government in which ideas, information, invention, and innovation are all open-sourced and accessible to all the people.

Imagine a state in which the public and private sectors are not seen as adversaries but each act in their own domains in the best interests of all the people and act as partners in domains where it is in the best interests of all the people.

Perry said, "Cher, Wynn, Angelo, and I are neither right- nor left-wingers. We think Libertarians and Progressives are partly right; yet totally wrong. The marketplace has a lot going for it but it can't meet all the needs of society. Joint action can preserve and enhance what we call the *common good* but big-government bureaucracies are not the answer either. The traditional liberal answer for everything is enhanced top-down government intervention. Libertarians say just leave things alone and the magic hand will write the answer. In our vision, the state and private citizens need to work in partnership."

Imagine a state government in which there are more voices and more choices; in which all the people have access to ongoing participation rather than only at election time; a government in which decisions are made from the bottom up and not left to a political class in close relations with the moneyed class.

Imagine a state in which all the people can act, through referendum, on all laws passed by the Legislature, as well as propose laws through initiatives.

153

Imagine a state in which all the people are involved in establishing state-budget priorities.

Cher said, "De Tocqueville had some relevant things to say about this, too, but I'll quote a more recent source instead. In his essay on 'Tech Crunch,' Tim O'Reilly states: 'Too often, we think of government as a kind of vending machine. We put in our taxes, and we get out services: roads, bridges, hospitals, fire brigades, police protection ... And when the vending machine doesn't give us what we want, we protest. Our idea of citizen engagement has somehow been reduced to shaking the vending machine.'"

Imagine a state government less influenced by money and the persuasion industry.

Perry spoke next. "I don't believe this next slide needs much commentary. Get the money and the lobbyists and the Super PACS out of our democracy."

Imagine a Legislature as an "Assembly of Your Peers," like our venerable jury system [and like NITH] with selection of representatives by lot.

Imagine a state without the burden of costly campaigns and elections but with full and ongoing participation by all the people.

Imagine representatives who are able to spend their time and focus their efforts on performing their constitutional duties rather than on fundraising and getting reelected.

Perry continued. "Taken together, these three ideas accomplish a number of things. The idea of sortition, or selection by lot, while controversial, has been tried and used. It was used in the Golden Age of Greece. It's used in our jury-selection system, a practice long honored in English law. Imagine the advantages—true government of all the people—of equality, access, inclusiveness, and fairness. Imagine the financial savings by avoiding costly campaigns and elections. Elections now cost millions of dollars to conduct, not including the millions each candidate spends to campaign for office. And, of course, the damn things go on forever. All in all, these three propositions go a long way toward taking the money out of politics.

"Now, our last slide."

> *Imagine a state in which city and other local governments are encouraged and supported in the creation of new forms and initiatives, consistent with the law as well as with the spirit of these propositions.*

"NITH is chartered by Governor Birnbaum to propose constitutional amendments," Perry said. "However, we don't have to *wait* to change how we govern ourselves. We can take these ideas and, starting tomorrow, make things happen. Some ideas came out of Michigan Speaks and smaller-scale trials are already under way. What we are proposing here is focused on our major cities—cities like Flint—cities in our state that despite years of economic recovery, are still suffering a downward fiscal spiral.

"The associate director and chief operating officer of the Michigan Municipal League has said, 'Our system's just broken. Property taxes have not kept pace with the growing economy. The financial stress is not good at any level but is worst in southeast Michigan.'

"US Supreme Court Justice Louis Brandeis famously said that our states could be 'laboratories of democracy.' In a famous case, he wrote: 'a state may, if its citizens choose, serve as a laboratory; and try novel social and economic experiments without risk to the rest of the country.'

"What we are saying here this morning is the same thing but at the city level. Cities do not have to wait for a new amendment to the state constitution to act. NITH needs to encourage these efforts." Glancing at Tom Samuels, Perry concluded, "Let me wrap this up with one last slide, a quote from guess who?"

> *"I cannot help fearing that men may reach a point where they look on every new theory as a danger, every innovation as a toilsome trouble, every social advance as a first step toward revolution, and that they may absolutely refuse to move at all."* —Alexis de Tocqueville

Wynn smiled. "I would only add that hierarchies are a fading legacy of a command-and-control mindset. I'll leave it at that, for now."

"Thanks, Wynn," said Perry. "You other guys have anything you want to add?"

They shook their heads. Angelo said, "No. I think you've covered it very well."

A smiling Lem Tracker said, "You've certainly given us a lot to *imagine*. Maybe we should hear the so-called minority report before we start discussions. Do we need a short break first?

Madeline Edges spoke up. "Mister chairman, I don't think that will be necessary. We're not going to need nearly as much time as Mr. Karas. I think we can squeeze in whatever we have to say before a break. I'll make this short and sweet. No fancy slides or music. Just common sense.

"Perry and his cohorts and their internet cloud are going to spiff up everything and transform the way government operates, complete with 100% transparency, one of the values this group says we embrace. I have my doubts that we really mean that. His specifics are few. Some of us might say, at this point of the morning, thank goodness for that. Even Wynn admits that no one has yet figured out a way to build stable government institutions based on his so-called peer-network ideas. All sizzle and no steak. They propose replacing our present form of democracy with a government by who knows? Qualifications not necessary; all solving their own problems in amorphous groupings. To me, this appears to be nothing less than the abdication of the legitimate duties of government."

Raising his hand, Tom Samuels said, "Amen."

Edges continued. "Our question is *why?* Our present constitution may need some tweaking here and there but why change our basic democratic system, one designed by men of courage and intellect and the genius of vision? This system has served our country for over two and half centuries and made America the greatest nation in the world. We propose that NITH tweak a few things, like the gerrymander system and voter fraud and leave the rest alone."

As she was winding down, Tom Samuels got out of his seat, went to the whiteboard, and began to print in large letters with a blue marking pen. He said, "I told Maddy she should present our case, and she has done a great job. But, with all those slides the other group put up, I thought we should have at least one visual aid of own." He turned around to face the group and laughed. On the board he had written:

If it ain't broke, don't fix it!

"That," he said, putting down the pen, "is *our* manifesto."

Madeline Edges smiled and said, "Okay. Now it's time for a break."

CHAPTER 23

Owens Meets NITH

As Angelo and Perry walked to the back of the conference room, Perry spotted Jimmy Owens of the *Free Press*. Owens, dressed in a casual sport coat, jeans, and athletic shoes, also had his eye on Perry. The two exchanged enthusiastic handshakes.

Perry said, "I thought we were getting together after lunch."

"Governor Birnbaum thought it would be okay for me to sit in on some of the meeting itself. Lana Hartman was supposed to let you know. I hope it's not a problem."

Perry glanced at his phone, which had been on silent during the session. He saw that Lana had left a text. "Sure, Jimmy, no problem. This is all supposed to be open and transparent anyway, right?"

"Right, and from what I've seen and heard so far, it's also pretty open in terms of ideas."

"You could say that," Perry answered. He turned to Angelo. "My friend Angelo RoundSky."

As they shook hands, Owens said, "Angelo RoundSky. That name rings a bell. Are you a hockey guy, too?"

"Once, a long time ago, but never like this guy," said Angelo.

"Now I remember. You were the young Native American phenom who burned up the juniors for Draytonware back in the day. I wrote a column about you."

"Didn't think you would remember," said Angelo. "I still have that column. But that's all ancient history."

"So, whatever happened? Where'd you end up?"

"A long, boring story. Let's just say my college coach and I didn't see the game the same way."

"That's too bad. I'd like to talk with you some more about it. Might make another column."

At that moment they were joined by Lem Tracker, whom Perry introduced as their moderator. "Tough job, I'll bet," said Owens.

"Not so bad," Tracker replied. "But I don't intend to make it a permanent position either. I'm with Angelo's ancestors—temps as chiefs. Especially when we get into topics like we just were. I have my own opinions and I may recuse myself as moderator so I can express them. Anyway, nice to meet you Mr. Owens. I'm a fan of your work. We were expecting you *after* lunch though."

Owens asked how Tracker thought the meeting was going.

"It's been lively. Most people are not bashful about sharing their points of view. Smart, too. When I think back to when we started just yesterday, it seems like forever ago; yet we're soon going to run out of time with so much left to do. We haven't been together very long, and we've had some ups and downs, but I think we're doing what we're supposed to do. I'm just honored to be a part of it."

"I'm impressed, I can tell you," said Owens. "I hope I made that clear in my column on Michigan Speaks."

Perry said, "Hope we can keep that going. When is Lana supposed to be here?"

"Right now," said Lana, pulling on Perry's sleeve from behind. "Hi, everybody. What have I missed?"

Jimmy Owens said, "You missed a good debate about the future of democracy."

"So, who won?" she asked.

Owens answered, "I'd say you made it just in time to hear the judges render their decision."

"The governor's coming. I'm sure he would like to hear that."

Angelo used the remainder of the break to take care of two necessities. After the long session, he had to pee and he wanted to check in with Lexi. "How are you doing, Mommy?"

Lexi said everything was fine. "Not any morning sickness yet, thank goodness. How about you? Tell me all about everything."

"Well, I don't quite have time for that, hon. Our twenty-minute break is almost over. We had quite a session first thing this morning. I think we're getting there, slowly but surely. One thing just happened that I could never have believed. I just met Jimmy Owens, the *Free Press* columnist. Do you know who I mean?"

"Of course. I have the column he wrote about you years ago pasted in the scrapbook I kept on you when you were that big-headed Eagletown sports hero."

"Well, he remembered me from that column! Can you believe that?"

"I'm not too surprised, my friend. You are just so memorable. But I don't want you to get that big head back."

"No chance, now with you are around. Listen, hon, I have to get back in there. I love you."

"Love you, babe. Have fun but not too much fun."

Angelo was still smiling when he reentered the meeting room. People were just getting in their seats. Lana and Jimmy Owens were about to sit in the back by themselves when Tracker invited them to join the group at the tables. "Knowing you two are here observing is strange enough, but we don't want you sitting back there like a panel of judges."

Lana took a seat on one side of the room and Owens across from her.

"Are you are choosing sides already?" Samuels said with a laugh.

"Totally objective" Jimmy Owens said. "You know me."

"As if," said Tracker, opening his laptop. "Ever heard of observer bias?"

"Ever heard of the Turing paradox?" asked Owens.

"Afraid not. Was that in the movie?" asked Tracker.

"Maybe," said Owens, "but I don't think so. It's sometimes called the quantum Zeno Effect. An unstable particle, if observed continuously, will never decay. So, if Lana and I continue to observe your discussions, they won't die. Nothing for you to worry about."

"That's exactly what we *are* worried about," said Samuels. "That these unstable discussions will never die; so thanks a lot."

"Okay, then Lana and I will just sit here as silent photons and see if we can keep from messing things up."

Tracker laughed and signaled he was ready to start. "Let's agree that it's nice to have these two here and get back to where we were. Which is where, exactly?"

"We had just finished the two reports on structure," said Lauren Bommarito. "And I confess, I am pulled in both directions—excited by the possibilities in Perry's and Cher's presentation, but I also see some pretty big risks. We really would be breaking the mold. I'm not sure we could figure out how to do it. I see Madeline's points too. It would be easier for us to tweak a few things. Maybe that's all we need to do. Is there a major problem in our present constitution? I'm ashamed to admit, I haven't read all of it yet."

Wayne Keith said, "I see risks either way. For sure there are risks in breaking the mold, just like Lauren says. And there are risks the other way too. It may feel safer to make minor changes but look at what's happening on the streets in our state and across the country. President Boykin and Governor Birnbaum may be polar opposites, but they were both elected to shake things up. If we come back with something that looks like business as usual, I can imagine the uproar."

"We do have some major problems," said Representative Susan Kerns. "Think about where we're sitting right now. Flint. Let's not forget Henry Ortega. We have problems with water, with pipeline risks, companies siphoning our water table for free and selling it back to us in bottles. More arid states would drain the Great Lakes at a minute's notice if they could."

"And that's just water," said Cher Richie. "We have the same broken electoral system as Washington, the same adversarial two-party system, the same lobbying system, the same overall systemic breakdown that leads to the same divisiveness and corruption. At least we have term limits—and Governor Birnbaum and this group."

Nick Lahti said, "So, let's not forget how we got here. This process was the governor's idea. Right, Lana? He's not looking for small tweaks. 'Small change is just what it is worth, small change.' Didn't he say that, or am I wrong?"

Lana smiled and nodded her head.

"I see one of the photons lighting up," said Martha Smith.

"So much for impartial observers," said Madeline Edges, managing a rueful smile.

Tom Samuels followed up. "It's easy to see the way this is going. The thing is, I'm not sure I can support what I'm hearing. Call me a tweaker if you want. I do not approve of making fundamental changes to our constitution. It might be better for everyone if I just resign from the group."

Perry immediately spoke up. "Please, don't, Tom. I'm sure you and Madeline are not the only ones who feel the way you do." Several heads nodded in agreement. "This democracy right here and now, our democracy in this room, needs to pay attention to all points of view. There's no progress without disagreement, unless we're talking about a utopia—and we aren't there yet."

"You could have fooled me; especially after this morning's session," said Edges. "What I heard sounded like an internet version of utopia."

'You're not all wrong," said Wynn. "A democracy based on peer networks will still be messy. But, like Oscar Wilde said: 'A map of the world that does not include utopia is not even worth consulting.'"

"Aha," laughed Holly Rifkin. "Caught you."

"I confess," said Wynn. "But I also bring realism to the table."

"Thank god," said Edges.

"Hold on here, folks," said Susan Kerns. "We are making progress but we have a long way to go. Even if we all buy into the idea of upsetting the apple cart, we are a long way from figuring out how to do it. There are a lot of unanswered questions. We can use everyone's input, no matter where you think you stand now. Wynn admits no one has invented a way to turn some of his ideas into stable government institutions. We need practical ideas, just like we need dreamers. I know *I* do in my new job."

"Here, here," said Perry. "Couldn't have said it better myself."

Angelo chimed in. "Some of you were interested in my Algonkian history. The spirits, as I said, don't dwell somewhere up in heaven. They're all around us. We believe they are not infallible rulers. They are no better or worse than us humans, with both strengths and weaknesses. Humans can tangle with the spirits and debate the spirits' actions and ideas. It is not only *okay* to tangle, but we are expected to. In these meetings, NITH will have many ideas to wrestle with. No one among us knows all the answers. I respect my brother Tom and my sister Madeline. I believe they are sincere people who want what's best for our state. I respect all my other brothers and sisters in this room. We are here to accomplish something important for the future of all of us. As many Natives believe, we must accomplish something for the next seven generations to come. We need all of our thinking and all of our ideas to accomplish that."

A long silence ensued. Finally, Tom Samuels broke the spell. "I guess that means I'll be staying."

There was a palpable sigh of relief in the room.

Lem Tracker said, "Thank you everyone for this discussion. I'll say again, I am honored to be a part of this group. Percy, I hope you got all that for your blog."

"Not all of it, I'm sure," he said. "I'll do my best to summarize."

Jimmy Owens asked, "Can I say something? I'd like to thank all of you for letting me sit in. It's been quite a morning and I look forward to listening to a few of you after lunch."

They addressed some last-minute business before they adjourned for the week, had lunch, and most headed home. Unlike the day before, the mood was positive. Governor Birnbaum joined them for lunch and was briefed by those at his table, which buoyed his spirits as well. His enthusiasm grew as he listened to the interviews with Owens.

Perry caught Angelo before they left. "Ang, I just want to wish you and Lexi all the best. Did I hear you say you plan to get married pretty soon?"

"You heard right. We were already starting to plan before this all happened. Lexi is all over it."

"I just wanted to let you in on something that I haven't told anyone else. Remember Dr. Majors, from the hospital in Flint?"

"Don't tell me …"

"Yep, we're engaged. But keeping it quiet for now. We hope to keep my little bit of celebrity out of it as long as we can. Maybe the four of us can get together some time."

CHAPTER 24

Monday's Free Press

Charlie Birnbaum was surprised to see that NITH had taken over the front page of his morning paper. The headline on Jimmy Owens' column at the top of the page, "Democracy Baby", was the last line of his previous column on the Michigan Speaks conference.

Owens' "Time Out" column normally appeared on Sundays, but there it was at the top of Monday's front page. The other lead story, on the right of the page, was an article by Darren Collender, the reporter who had quoted the two state Legislative leaders who coined the phrase "Charlie Birnbaum's Hail Mary." In a shaded box across the bottom of the page was Percy Oliver's report of the weekend meeting.

Owens extolled NITH and the process he had observed the day before in Flint. He praised the openness; the eagerness to put forward new ideas; and the willingness to confront disagreement, "even to the point of encouraging it," he wrote. "And yet to do so with civility and sometimes even good-natured humor." He described "innovative, out-of-the-box thinking," beginning with the verse from John and Yoko's "Imagine" that Perry Karas had used in his presentation. Other ideas Karas had outlined included transparency, peer-to-peer networks, and selecting representatives by lot. Owens emphasized the trust-in-government issue. He quoted NITH participants, including Madeline Edge, when she said, "I don't agree with everything, but that's as it should be, don't you think?"

"Democracy, baby."

Charlie stopped smiling when he started to read the Collender piece. Lana and he had sensed goodwill in their meeting with Jarrett and Risen. *That didn't last long*, the governor thought as he read:

> Anonymous sources close to the leadership of the minority Republican Party in both the state House and Senate are challenging the legality of the whole amendment process. The current constitution called for the possibility of a constitutional Convention only every sixteen years, several years in the future. "The kinds of amendments under discussion," Collender reported, "could change the underlying foundation of the constitution itself. It is unclear that this process is even legal."

> Then there is the issue of the 'guarantee' clause of our US Constitution ...

Article Four. Charlie knew it. "The United states shall guarantee to every state in this Union a Republican Form of Government."

On his way into the office, Birnbaum phoned Lana from the backseat of the limo. "I hope you didn't read the good news first, like I did," he told her.

"I did. Top of the page. Why?"

"Better to get the good news last. Makes for a nicer day."

"Maybe you're right. That Article Four crap really pissed me off. Nobody even knows what that clause means, not even the Supreme Court."

"They've mostly treated it as irrelevant or refer it to Congress," Charlie said. "And, I know from what you've told me that NITH is doing nothing that could violate that clause."

"Absolutely," said Lana. "NITH may be talking about different means for selecting representatives, but it's still a representative form of government with the people as the selectors. That's what the Guarantee Clause calls for. Article Four is in the constitution to prevent states from deciding to have a monarchy. If there is anything the NITH people are *not* considering, it's that. More direct democracy, not less. That's their vision."

"Which is *not* prohibited by Article Four," Birnbaum said. "Madison and company may not have been big fans of it, but they never argued that the exercise of direct democracy by the states should be banned."

Lana said, "It's just a smoke screen by Jarret and company. They're thumping their chests."

"And Janice Risen and her Dems?"

"Lord protect us from those who would damn us with faint praise," Lana said. Birnbaum heard a newspaper rattle over the phone. Lana read: "'Democratic Speaker of the House Janice Risen defended the NITH project by saying that they are a group of sincere, dedicated laymen who should be granted some slack.'

"How about *that* for strong support?"

Charlie looked out the window at the well-tended grounds of the gubernatorial estate. He rubbed his chin.

Lana continued to read. "'I am fully on board with our governor's efforts at reform and this group of well-intentioned citizens is a major part of that effort, so I'm behind it. Of course, that doesn't mean we have to buy every proposal that they produce. The separation of powers is still in effect the last time I looked.'"

Lana said, "Thank you for that, Speaker Risen. To repeat an old cliché, keep your enemies close and your friends closer."

"Exactly."

"Did you see Percy Oliver's progress report?" Lana asked.

"Not yet," said the governor, as he skimmed the article, nodded to himself, and said, "Looks fine. As a balanced, matter-of-fact summary. Nothing controversial. You need to email him and thank him."

"I will. He already posted the summary as a blog. We should be getting citizen feedback on it."

Charlie sat back and laughed. "So, you got a whole page of publicity," he said. "Front page at that. Some of it wasn't so good. *Succès de scandale*, as they say."

"No such thing as bad publicity. Want me to dig in on the legal stuff?" Lana asked.

"I'll ask my counsel if there's even anything that needs digging into. What I see is a lot of smoke and no fire. Just another hurdle."

As soon as he arrived at the office, his admin, Rosa, told Charlie that Darren Collender was waiting on the line, if he wanted to talk with the reporter.

"Hell, yes. Put him on."

"Governor Birnbaum? Thank you for taking my call. This is Darren Collender. I don't suppose you are eager to talk with me this morning."

"That story obviously won't help, but I know you're just doing what you see as your job."

"But not the way *you* see my job?"

"It doesn't really matter now, does it? What can I do for you?"

"I'm just reaching out to you and Lana Hartman for a statement. I called both of you before I filed the article but couldn't get through."

"So you said in the article."

"Still trying."

"I don't think I want to comment right now."

"Okay. But Governor, I want you to know I am really not out to undermine you or this process. I wrote about what came my way. You read Jimmy's column. I can't personally dispute anything he wrote. We're obviously getting two different sides of the story. I would be glad to get yours."

"Nice to know, Mr. Collender. We'll stay in touch."

"Sure thing. Have a good day."

Charlie hung up and immediately called Lana back, filling her in on his conversation with the reporter. "We need to get ahead of this story. Take Collender up on his offer, for one thing. I'll also get my PR people working on it. We need to get the word on the front page, not in a correction paragraph buried on page four. I'll have my people work something up, but we have to go bigger. We have to approach this thing like an election campaign. We need to tend to the politicos, and I should also be out there visibly selling it to the public. The pols need to know that the public is with us."

"So, get your press release out there," Lana said. "Talk to the Freep creep, say whatever you think is right, but let's set up a major news conference as soon as we can. A campaign it is. We both know how to do that. But let's not get sucked in by Collender's offer. As my wonderful, staunch-Reagan-supporter grandfather loves to quote, 'Trust but verify.' In this case, we may have to verify before we trust. But anyway, you and I are on the same page. In the meantime, I'll get started on the press conference idea."

"We could also have some of the NITH people there."

"The people who talked with Jimmy Owens?"

"Fine, but it can't look like a setup. We're not cherry picking."

"I'm going to call and thank Jimmy."

"I should do the same."

"I'll keep him looped in all the way, Charlie."

"Find some friends and light some fires, I always say."

"We need more friends at the moment."

"Never enough friends. Love you, Lana."

Next, Charlie checked out the NITH blog. He was stunned to read the first entry in the comment section:

```
What the hell is going on here?
We have a so-called process spon-
sored and supported by our rad-
ical socialist governor, led by
a radical lesbian lawyer who is
a university academic lefty, and
who sleeps with a lesbian aborig-
inal from Australia. The group
```

called by the ridiculous name of NITH is chaired by a black college kid, filled with Indians just let off the reservation, a Muslim woman in a hijab and other blacks like the lefty academic who wrote this report. Oh, yes, I almost forgot, one of the group's leaders is a dumb jock hockey player who has had his head banged around at least one too many times. This flotsam and jetsam is not my Michigan. This pond scum is not my America. They do not represent me. And they are seriously considering taking away my right to vote. Say no to these radicals. Say no to NITH.

CHAPTER 25

Feedback

For Charlie Birnbaum, keeping up with the media prior to the press conference was like trying to maneuver through rush-hour traffic. It was stop and go congestion. The *Free Press* even dedicated a whole page to accommodate Letters to the Editor just on NITH.

Feedback overwhelmed the NITH blog, website, and Facebook page; fortunately, it was mostly positive. Lana told Charlie that emails, text messages, and Tweets were jamming her computer and cellphone. Political blogs went crazy, and mainstream news outlets just tried to keep up, in the state and nationally. It was the story of the week.

It was difficult for the governor to judge the winners versus the losers. Lana told him she always focused on the voices of the opposition. As a Senate aide, she knew how to count votes, she said, and those against her man always hit home harder than those with him. She cited comments to Charlie like: *"Too much too soon." "Dreamers." and "We could easily get unqualified people running our government."* She admitted to Charlie that she shared some of those concerns herself.

RICHARD AULT

"Naturally," he said. "All those ideas from NITH are still only provisional, tentative. It's too early for vote counting. But how about the positive comments?"

She acknowledged themes like: *"He's keeping his campaign promise." "It's about time somebody is actually addressing our broken system." "We need to get back to a true democracy." And "I look forward to trusting my state government again."*

And they shared their disgust with the hardcore trolls who said things like: *"Bunch of communists/socialists/fascists; stupid assholes; where do they come up with these dumb ideas?"*

Lana summed it up for Charlie this way: Their base was strongly with them. They had made progress with those in the middle and the formerly undecided. And the naysayers were not about to give up.

She found it easier to dismiss the trolls than the thoughtful critics. She had doubts of her own but knew the process itself would take care of those, at least some of them. Still she was nervous about Friday's meeting with the media.

One thing gnawed at both of them: the noise out of Washington. Boykin and his henchmen had laughed off what he Tweeted as "the Birnbaum fiasco"—from the early days of Charlie's campaign right up to and including the Tweets of the morning: *"Crackpot scheme. Not even constitutional We won his state by a huge margin and he still doesn't get it. Let him have his fun."*

And: *It's going to be disaster, I guarantee you, a guaranteed disaster, you wait and see."*

And: *"More important things to worry about. So-called governor of Michigan not even on my radar."*

It was typical Boykin stuff.

Lana briefed Charlie on the underground rumblings that some of the White House, maybe even members of Michigan's Congressional delegation, including Senator Billings, were quietly causing to undermine things. Birnbaum's staff and Lana were doing their best to track all this but were mostly still in the dark.

The governor registered all the negatives in a straightforward way, but tried, in his disarming style, to lift Lana's spirits. Most of the prep for the press conference was being competently handled by the governor's staff, but he was glad some details were left for Lana, to help take her mind off the turbulence.

She said she wanted to make sure the NITH team was well informed and cared for. Charlie told her to invite the members who would be at the conference to gather in his inner office a few minutes before it began. "Then," he said, "let's have them and their significant others for a big dinner celebration afterwards." At a minimum he hoped it would be a celebration of a public relations success and, at best, a political breakthrough.

The governor enjoyed giving the group a tour of his inner office. He discovered that for most, it was the first time they had ever seen such a "seat of power." They looked like tourists as they checked everything out. The office was reasonably large, in keeping with the prestige of the office, but not palatial. It was his workplace. He had stopped in the middle of some paperwork the moment they arrived, leaving marked up papers open on his desk. He just smiled as people checked out his handwritten notes in the margins; the same with other working papers on the small conference table where he held private meetings. He explained pieces of memorabilia on the shelves, giving the backstory to each. He was most proud when he showed off the framed family photos—his son in uniform, for example, the West Point grad now a Special Forces officer wearing his beret; his youngest daughter about to start Yale Law School; the group photos of his grandchildren, one of whom had her own separate framed picture of her caught in the process of making a kill for her high school volleyball team.

"That's how she got a scholarship to Purdue," he said with a glow. "She's started every game since she was a freshman—near the top of the Big Ten in kills. She's studying engineering."

Once everyone had a chance to nose around, Charlie welcomed them more officially and told them how proud he was of the work they were doing. "Don't worry about the negative stuff," he said, "you are doing exactly what I hoped—knocking around a lot of ideas, including some new ones that take some people by surprise. Sometimes it takes people a while to get their heads around new ideas before they make sense, and, for some, of course, that time never comes. But at this point, your work is right where it should be—open-ended. You're just getting started, but it was a great start. I hope you know that.

"As to what's going to happen next," he said, "who knows? I'm sure we'll get some tough questions from the press, that's their job. But I think between all of us, we can handle it. I'm actually looking forward to it—and I can't always say that before a press conference. In this case, we've got a good story to tell and that's all we have to do—make sure we tell our story, no matter what they throw at us.

"This session could go a long way to building public support for your work, which will help us get the political support we're going to need. I'm not at all nervous about it; just excited, and I hope you are too. I'm certainly counting on you to tell it like it is."

He shook hands all around and showed an interest in each person and his or her own personal stories; then it was time to go out to his larger ceremonial office. The press was waiting.

CHAPTER 26

Meet the Press

Governor Birnbaum took his place at the podium; Lana stood next to him while NITH members sat in chairs on either side. He smiled the Birnbaum smile and paused to take a long drink of water before welcoming the reporters.

"I want everyone to see the faces and hear the actual voices of NITH firsthand. This is not just another faceless group, off somewhere making decisions and coming up with plans that affect the lives of other people. These are real people, not a bunch of politicians or bureaucrats, as is all too often the case."

Lana introduced them from her right to left—Percy Oliver, Tom Samuels, Perry Karas, Angelo RoundSky, Susan Kerns, Cher Richie, Wayne Keith, and Lem Tracker. She stressed their diversity in background, geography, gender, race, and ethnicity. "Most importantly," she emphasized," is the diversity in their ideas and points of view." The same could be said, she claimed, of all twenty-five NITH members. "We did not stack the deck especially for you or this conference. These folks were chosen by NITH members to speak for the subgroups that are working on several important topics."

The governor thanked Lana and then continued with his opening remarks. "My personal thanks go out to all the members of this team. This is not just a Charlie Birnbaum show; although, make no mistake, Charlie Birnbaum is all in and happy to be here." He then acknowledged the naysayers. "Those of you in the media," he said, "know that conflict makes for a better story than harmony and agreement. I get that. I fully expect there will be conflict until we have approved and implemented a new amendment or two. And *still* we will have conflict. It may quiet down some as things settle but it will never go away.

"We are not bothered by the concerns expressed over the last week. And we are heartened by the responses to the first NITH report. What we object to, object to most forcefully, are the nasty, obscene, threatening, and thoughtless—without an ounce of thought or reason—commentary on some of the social media sites. I'm sure you see that too, in your own work. These folks live among us. That tone of discourse bothers the hell out of me—but that's the world we live in.

"We want to make changes in our state government. We want to replace our current system with something different—a true democracy. That promise was the central theme of my campaign for governor. That's why the voters elected me. That also got President Boykin elected. By now, though, people of all political persuasions can appreciate the differences in how he and I think about what we need to do.

"Somebody once told me 'if you change enough of the

little pictures, you end up changing the big picture.' I believe that to be true. Michigan Speaks set in motion experiments with small changes. A village in the Upper Peninsula began selecting its Village Council by lot. Radical as that idea appears to some, the residents of that community are happy with the results so far. It has also been tried in a Detroit subdivision, where they chose their latest homeowners association the same way. Any of you ever tried to work with a homeowner's association? I'd rather work with our state Legislature! Yes, they can be nasty but nothing like a homeowners group. Of course, that experiment is just underway and the jury is still out. Should be fun to follow.

"Other small-scale efforts have sprung up as a result of the conference. Some factory organizations and white-collar offices are engaged in innovative practices to increase dignity, meaning, and a sense of community in the workplace. Some of these attempts are not so small-scale. Then, there are the water protectors, led by the Native tribes of this state, but also including people from all walks of life, acting to protect our fresh waters. Volunteer networks working to help the people of Flint, from lawyers engaged in pro bono efforts to everyday folks helping neighborhoods with their water and health issues. This work was going on before, but it has increased considerably since Michigan Speaks. Perry Karas, Lamarcus Townsend, and Dr. Julia Majors of the Hurley Hospital Pediatric Center, have started a promising foundation called Henry's Helpers, to make health education and health resources available in Flint community schools.

"Speaking of education, a peer network has been formed to look at our entire statewide system of school finance. Communities are enacting citizen participation in budgeting. Everyday citizens get together in meeting halls and school gyms to draft their budget priorities. The mayor of a small town in the central part of the Lower Peninsula—a man who was at Michigan Speaks—declared his goal is for his town to be the happiest place to live in the state—not the most prosperous or the prettiest—but the happiest. People-to-people efforts at inclusion have moved my heart.

"While I am pleased with these efforts, I did not run on small-scale change. I promised to change the big picture. For the big picture to change, the little pictures have to be visible. How many of *you* knew about the things I just shared? If you *did* know, did you report on them? Would your outlets publish or air those reports? When incremental improvements do not get covered, no one else learns from them and they do not spread. Even the innovations that don't work out are not failures if we learn from them—but we can't learn if we don't even know about them.

"I am not condemning the media for that," he added. "It's just the nature of the beast. Negative makes better headlines, reading, and viewing. You and I are not going to change that today. We just have to accept that's the way it is and move on. But, the good news out there is crying for attention.

"We also know that large systems of all kinds, whether it's one of the Big Three automakers or our state government, have an almost infinite ability to absorb new inputs without any substantial change to the system itself. If you want substantive change, you have to come at it with more than enough resources and from more than enough directions that it can't soak up anymore, that you reach a tipping point. I guess a nuclear scientist might speak of reaching a point of critical mass when a chain reaction takes place and there is no stopping it. To do that, you need to change the frame of the picture, create a new context. As you have heard me say time and time again, it is not enough to change the people, we need to change the game.

"Changing the game is why I ran for governor and that's what I intend to do, with the help of the good people you see up here and the rest of their colleagues, and with the help of our Legislature and the good people of this great state. Thank you. Let's have some questions."

"What about the blowback?" someone asked.

"It's true there has been some negative response. But that is democracy at work, the kind of democracy I'm seeking, in fact. Most of the people who are raising questions and objections are conscientious citizens. They care about the future of their state. Maybe some of those comments come from our 'loyal opposition.' We need to pay attention to all of the concerns. By 'we' I mean the people you see up here this afternoon and their NITH colleagues.

"If you read Percy Oliver's report in the blog, you will know NITH members did not agree on everything. Some members raised their concerns strongly and candidly. This was their first meeting. No one expected final results from a first meeting on issues as important as these. Every idea, every proposal, and every viewpoint and opinion expressed is still tentative. So, for now, everyone should just relax and give these folks some time."

Percy Oliver chimed in. "When I wrote my report,

I had to weigh how much to write about any disagreements. We had a lot of good vibes in the room, and there were also ups and downs. I decided to tell it like it was, so I am not surprised or at all discouraged by the blowback. I would not have expected anything else."

"We are all big boys and girls," said Tom Samuels. "We are not going to let a few negative comments stop us. Bring it on."

The governor pointed out that the blowback was also coming from politicians. He found Darren Collender, the *Free Press* reporter and said, "As for how we deal with our loyal opposition, that's just good, old-fashioned politics. We need people from all political points on the compass, and we will seek them out. We are meeting with our legislators from both sides of the aisle. Some of my fellow governors have been in contact. They are watching us closely. Some, I think, like what they see.

"Remember Judge Brandeis's well-known opinion about states being laboratories for new ideas and innovation. That is precisely what Michigan is doing, and governors in other states are also trying some of their own ideas. In this period of general and great disruption, the time is ripe for trying new things.

"We will need other states to innovate their governments. New practices do not last long if they are isolated. I am doing my best to involve a network of other governors in following the Brandeis principle. We can learn from them and they can learn from us. I have great hopes that states, given the present level of tumult, will be seen even more as incubators of innovation. Now is the time.

"As for our friend in Washington, until the publicity of the last week, the administration hadn't paid much attention to us. If they saw us at all, it was just as another state periodically reviewing its constitution. Our President, poor guy, has a lot more to worry about than us—like whether or not he's going to have a job. And Congress? The House and the Senate have been quiet up to now, as well. I'm keeping our Michigan delegation informed and have asked them for input. Senator Hatherly and I ran on the same platform this last election, as did some of our representatives. Senator Billings came in with Boykin, which means he has some dilemmas within his own party. I continue to keep him in the loop as well though. By the time we have something finalized, my hope is that he will see a way to support what's best for his state."

When a reporter questioned the notion of random selection of representatives, Birnbaum turned to Perry Karas, who said he had first heard the word *sortition* from his Greek grandmother. He had studied the concept for years.

"There were other ways of doing business than the one we use now," Karas explained. "Sortition served not only Greece but other civilizations, and more recently has been used by other countries involved in political reform. So it isn't really new and revolutionary. It would have some obvious advantages but, as Governor Birnbaum said, we are just in the early stages here, throwing out ideas, discussing possibilities. We don't want to get ahead of ourselves."

Governor Birnbaum added, "How about no more lengthy and costly campaigns? Just think of the money we would save, including all the dark money and the influence of big money in general. And, without the campaigns, people like you and me would have to find more productive things to do. We could both focus on serious issues, like what's best for the people of our state."

A reporter directed a question to Susan Kerns. "How do *you* feel about that, after recently spending a great deal of effort and, I'm sure, money, to get elected to your first term?"

She smiled. "Ask my husband that question! If it were up to him, we would have retired by now to live near our son and his family on Walloon Lake. I had amazing support, financial and otherwise, by the people of my district, but fundraising was hard and we had to use too much of our own savings. I'm grateful for the opportunity to serve, make no mistake. But if I can make a contribution as a part of NITH, toward a democracy built on trust, I will have accomplished all I could have ever hoped for when I ran for office. If that means losing this job I just got, then watch out Walloon Lake and grandkids! Here we come—happily."

In a follow-up that evoked some laugher, the governor was asked if he would still have a job. Laughing, he said, "Who knows? Maybe I'll ride off into the sunset with Jacquie and enjoy retirement, satisfied that I contributed to a better democracy. Or, we may join Susan and her husband on that beautiful lake."

A reporter stood. "George Blakely, NBC, sir. Governor Birnbaum, no one, so far, has raised what I think is the obvious and critical issue with what you call *sortition*. Voting is seen by many as the cornerstone of democracy. It's sacrosanct. You are promising a more democratic system; yet you would be taking that sacred, democratic privilege away."

Birnbaum winked at Perry Karas. "Thank you for that question, George. As my Greek friend over here will tell you, Aristotle would have disagreed with your statement. Tell him, Perry."

Perry responded. "Sortition was accepted practice in Athens during Aristotle's time. He is quoted as saying, 'It is accepted as democratic when public offices are allocated by lot; and as oligarchic when they are filled by election.' By the same token, the ruler himself, Pericles, said in his famous funeral oration for the war dead, 'It is administered by the many instead of the few; that is why it is called a democracy.'"

Birnbaum continued the explanation. "More democracy, not less—you hear that, George? Thank you, Perry. But, we don't need to go back that far in history to answer your question, or to philosophers. We have some recent and real examples right here in America. Many would say we already have an oligarchy, but let's put that aside and talk about our election process. Think back to the 2000 Presidential election. I'm not talking about who won and who lost, I'm talking about the election process itself. You spoke of sacrosanct. How sacred was it to have our democracy dependent on hanging chads, on lawyers blaming the other side, on a politicized Supreme Court making the final decision? And, what about our last election, in 2016? The ugly name-calling in the primary debates, which grew worse during the campaign itself—and continues to this day? The digging for dirt on both candidates? The possibility of foreign meddling in our election itself? The fact that in both 2000 and 2016, the so-called losing candidate won the popular vote? Sacrosanct? Maybe, if you mean many people cling to the idea religiously despite the reality of it. We know we have a job of education and persuasion to do. But sacred? No.

No way. More democratic? No way. Oligarchy? In my view and in the view of many, we are close to that now—if not already there.

"And, speaking of sacred, our jury system is pretty sacred too, even sacrosanct, you might say. It's every bit as much a part of our American system and values as our elections. George, let me ask *you* a question. In fact, I'll ask it of everyone in this room. Let's just suppose, hypothetically, that you, any one of you, is accused of a serious crime of which you are innocent. You genuinely did not do it. You are then granted the choice between being tried by a jury of your peers or by the United states Congress. Which do you choose? Having been a congressman for many years myself, I know what my answer would be. I know that if it were left up to Congress, you would immediately become a political football. Each party would be looking to score points at the expense of the other party and, most likely, at your expense as well. Your guilt or innocence would scarcely be of interest or concern.

"I dislike having to speak that way of my old institution, but I guarantee you that is what would happen. Now, I know juries are not perfect either. People on juries have their own prejudices and biases. There's even jury tampering. But, if a fair judgement is what we are after, give me a jury of my peers over Congress every time. How about you, George?"

The NBC reporter joined the general laughter in the room.

Finally, a reporter threw the bomb everyone expected. "Governor, despite your arguments for random selection, the NITH group itself has received some fairly virulent criticism about its makeup. One commenter called it

flotsam and jetsam, and another called it pond scum
Any comment?"

"I'm not about to comment on such bilge."

Angelo stood and moved to the podium. "Governor, if
it's okay, as what that troll called the "Indian just off the
reservation", I'd like to respond. The person who wrote
that comment specifically said that I do not represent
him or her. That's true. It is also true that I am a Native
American and proud of it. It is also true that I live on a
reservation in Eagletown. But, just as I do not represent
the person who wrote that vile stuff, I do not represent
the people on my reservation either. I only represent
myself—that's what we were told was our responsibility
when we selected to be a part of Michigan Speaks. We
were there as persons, as ourselves. Myself is made up of
many things. Native is part of who I am, I am proud to
say, but I am also a man, an American, a soon-to-be husband and father. One of the most important things I am
about is our Mother Earth—our landscape.

"If I represent anything at all in NITH, I represent the
landscape of our state and, for that matter, our planet.
The landscape does not hate. The earth knows no prejudice. As a human being, as a Native American, I once
knew hate and prejudice against the white man. But now
I see myself as part of the life of the earth and the round
sky and the great waters. I feel no hate and no prejudice. My favorite thing to do is to stand at the crest of
the great Sleeping Bear Dunes, either alone or with my
fiancé, Lexi, and look out over Lake Michigan and try to
see Wisconsin. We all know that's impossible. And that
is the very reason I do it. When I try to see Wisconsin,
I am really trying to see *beyond* the horizon, to see and

feel the earth's curvature, to sense the whole of the world. Everything I do or say in our NITH meetings is aimed at ensuring that that landscape is there my children. For your children.

"My ancestors and elders say we should always think seven generations ahead. I want the people, *all* the people seven generations ahead of us, to have the opportunity to look out from a cliff or mountaintop and try to see the world. Every issue we discuss in NITH has a bearing on that—the way we govern, the way we educate our young, the way we manage our economy, and the way we manage our environment. Everything we address will have an effect on the next seven generations. If you or the person who wrote that comment want to know who or what I represent, you can say I represent *two* things: I represent our home, the earth, and I represent the next seven generations."

While Angelo returned to his seat, Governor Birnbaum stood at the podium in silence, looking down as if looking at his notes, but there were no notes. Looking up, he quietly said, "Thank you, Angelo. And thank you, ladies and gentlemen."

CHAPTER 27

Celebration

Before the press conference, Perry and Julia had joined Angelo and Lexi for lunch. Lexi and Julia gave the guys a hard time when the men drove off in Perry's crimson Buick SUV, leaving Lexi to drive the truck for their afternoon of Lansing mall shopping. They agreed to meet back at the Kellogg Center to get ready for the dinner celebration.

When Angelo returned to their room at the Kellogg Center after the press conference, Lexi was waiting. "How did it go?" she asked.

"Well, I think," said Angelo. "The governor did a good job and the news people seemed satisfied. But all that is kind of out of my league."

"You've played in all kinds of leagues. You can play in this one."

"Not that you're prejudiced."

She was dressed for the dinner and he thought she looked just smashing. The dinner was business casual, but Lexi was a knockout, baby bump and all, in a warm-brown knit dress topped off by her amber-beaded necklace and shining black hair.

"How did it go with you and Julia after Perry and I left?"

"We shopped. She helped me pick out this dress."

"You look good enough to eat in that dress."

"Not right now, if you please. I'm ready but you need a shower. Anyway, we shopped a while and talked, then came back to our rooms to rest. I seem to need that more these days."

"Shopping, talking, or resting?"

"Rest, you idiot. But maybe some talk too. It was nice to have a new friend to talk to. She's a little down right now about her parents. They are not as happy about Perry as she hoped they would be."

"Really? She couldn't find a better catch. Is it racial?"

"I don't think so. Her parents are mixed race themselves. Her dad is black and her mother white. Julia adores them both and they feel the same about her. But they have concerns about her marrying a man younger than she is and with less education than she has."

"That's crazy."

"It surprised her too. She said they talked it through. She has hopes that they will get over it, but it's weighing on her."

Angelo climbed into the shower. While the water ran over his head and down his body, he realized that he was feeling some tension from the conference. He took a deep breath with a long exhale and tried to shrug it off and let it wash away. The afternoon was good but it was over. The press conference had been exhilarating, but this was just the beginning. It was going to be a long slog.

His mind turned to Lexi's comments about Julia and her parents, and another realization hit him. Lexi seemed tired, even a bit subdued. Gauging subtle changes in people's emotions was not one of Angelo's strong suits, so maybe he was wrong. He wondered if it was his impending fatherhood and smiled at the idea. He closed his eyes and tried to relax and focus on his breathing, but his mind raced back to the bluff on North Manitou.

When he came out of the bathroom, Lexi was watching the local news. Of course, they were reporting on the governor's news conference, probably bigger news on the local Lansing channel than it might have been elsewhere. The station played clips of Birnbaum's opening remarks and some highlights of the Q & A, including some of his fellow NITH members. Angelo was surprised when *he* appeared on the screen. He had never been on television before, except for some game video he had to watch in team film sessions. It was like watching and listening to someone else. The selected fragments of his comments actually embarrassed him. *Did I really say that? Do I really sound like that?*

The reporter's commentary was positive; then the focus shifted to man/woman on the street interviews; again mostly positive. A middle-aged woman in a Tigers shirt said she still had questions. A young man, probably a college student, said he was hopeful but would have to wait and see. Then they interviewed a couple state legislators, one from each party. Both were careful and polite about Birnbaum. His poll numbers were high enough to be intimidating. They avoided going on the record about where they stood on changes to the constitution.

Angelo found the coverage generally lukewarm—but at least it was warm. He said as much to Lexi.

"*You* weren't lukewarm. You were *hot*. You were sincere

and passionate. The man I know and love. But you didn't tell the whole Manitou story."

"I don't ever intend to. That's just between you and me and the eagles." He then turned his full attention to her. "You okay, Lex? You seem a bit down."

"Watching you on the news was exciting. This is going to be fun. But you're right, I have been a little nervous. Maybe it's the baby. I hope everything goes well at dinner."

"Why would there be any trouble? If there was going to be trouble, it would have been this afternoon. Tonight is just a celebration."

"I know, and it'll be fine, I'm sure. But you know me, I sometimes worry when I shouldn't."

"But too often you are right when you worry. That's what's got *me* worried now."

"Forget it. It's probably just the baby—hormones and all that stuff. I'm fine. And looking forward to the celebration."

Lexi and Angelo could hear the buzz the moment they got off the elevator. There was a mob in the hallway around the bar and the hors d'oeuvres table. Lana was holding court at the edge of the bar, a glass in her hand. She reached out and pulled Angelo toward her. "Great job today. You had people spellbound. Lexi, you look beautiful. Baby okay?"

"I'm fine," she said, pointing to her baby bump. "We're fine. I *am* a little nervous. I don't often find myself having dinner with a governor." She took Angelo's arm. "I'm so proud of my man."

Charlie approached and greeted the three of them with

his winning smile. "Great day, don't you think? Even Jacquie says so, and she's usually my toughest critic."

"I think we accomplished what we set out to do, sir," said Lana. She shook the governor's wife's hand. "I'm glad you agree, Jacquie."

Mrs. Birnbaum said. "You're his secret weapon, Lana."

The happy half hour stretched into forty-five minutes. Everybody was in good spirits and the noise level high. Finally, the governor called out, "Let's all go in and sit down. No standing on ceremony tonight. We're just here to have fun. Sit wherever you like."

The tables were set in rounds of eight chairs. Charlie and Jacquie Birnbaum took their place and Lana sat on Jacquie's left. At the next table were Angelo and Lexi with Perry and Julia.

The governor rose. "No speeches, tonight, folks. We had a good day. We didn't expect to hit any home runs. We all need to keep grinding. I *do* think we got in some solid singles and I think we may have loaded the bases. Now, we need to get some runs home. Okay, enough sports metaphors. I just want to thank all you NITH folks for your help today. It's nice to have a chance to meet your partners and thank them too. Now, let's eat and enjoy the night."

Angelo and Lexi were enjoying their fresh Lake Michigan whitefish. Others at their table commented on the high quality of the cuisine. None of the usual talk of institutional rubber chicken. Someone said the kitchen may have raised their game because of the governor's presence.

The dominant topic of conversation was their satisfaction with how the press conference had gone. "Angelo,

Perry tells me you were the most impressive of them all," Julia said.

"Awesome," said Lem Tracker.

Perry said, "Not the goon anymore, my friend. You scored big time."

A few people popped over from other tables with similar praise. He saw others nod his way and smile or give him a thumbs-up. Angelo was uncomfortable with the compliments. Head down, he murmured his thanks. Lexi beamed.

When the dessert was brought in, Angelo and Lexi were looking over at the governor's table. They laughed when he took a serving of the crème brûlé despite Jacquie shaking her head.

At that moment, a man wearing traditional chef's gear—a toque blanche and double-breasted white coat, entered the room. Angelo assumed it was the cook coming out to greet his guests and take his bows. People began to applaud in appreciation. As he approached the governor's table, Birnbaum smiled, rose, and reached to shake the man's hand.

Instead of taking the governor's hand, the man quickly reached under his chef's coat and pulled out a handgun.

Angelo felt Lexi's scream before he heard it. In virtually a single motion, he pushed her under the table and dived at the man, knocked him to the floor, causing both shots to go off their mark. Yet, one stuck the Governor. Another Jacquie.

From the table to the right, Tom Samuels also dived at the assailant. He wrested the Glock 42 from the man's hand. Between Angelo's hockey fighting instincts and Samuels's military training, the man didn't stand a chance. Security personnel took over. While two tended to the wounded couple, others took control of the situation and waved everyone else away.

After her initial shocked reaction, Julia Major's instincts kicked in. She pulled away from Perry's grip.

"Please, I'm a doctor," she shouted. She rushed to care for the governor, who seemed the more seriously injured of the two.

Around the dining room, people had dropped to their knees or run for the exits. Husbands threw themselves on top of their wives. Others gawked, too stunned to move. Some looked around to see if there were other possible perpetrators.

The security guards handcuffed the man and hustled him out of the room. On his way out, he shouted, *"Radical! Traitor! Commie! What you're doing is treason!"* The last words he yelled as he was shoved out the door was "Pond scum!"

Even though Angelo's ears rang from the shots, he could hear Lana doing her best to comfort Mrs. Birnbaum. "Charlie's okay, Jacquie. He's going to be fine." Angelo was not so sure and guessed Lana shared his doubts.

Angelo was on edge. He hankered to fight someone else in the worst way. There were no more comers. He went to Lexi, who was still under the table, crying. "This was it, wasn't it?" he asked. "You knew something was up."

"I didn't know anything. I just knew I felt something." He held her as she stood and cried into his shoulder.

Other couples clung together. The adrenaline had peaked. Now drained, people were confused and at a loss.

Angelo let go of Lexi. He made his way in the direction of the prone governor. He was not allowed to get too close. Julia was giving directions to the security detail. Angelo could see blood on Birnbaum's shirt. His eyes were open and alert; they looked angry. He stared straight at Angelo as if to challenge him.

"Don't worry, sir. We'll keep fighting. We'll get your victory."

"The people, Angelo. Fight for the people's victory ... and fuck that guy and any others like him."

"Yes, sir."

The Governor closed his eyes.

PART THREE

PART THREE

CHAPTER 28

The Morning After

Angelo slept little the night of the assassination attempt. Early the next morning, careful not to wake Lexi, he eased his way out of the room. He picked up a copy of the *Lansing State Journal* on his way into the Kellogg Center's breakfast room. The cafe was eerily quiet as the other guests also read the paper or conversed in hushed tones. The waitstaff was equally subdued. Angelo read as he ate.

Of course, the front page carried news of the assassination attempt, those stories and others on the subject continued on the inside as well as on the editorial page. The governor had sustained a gunshot wound in his right lung, which collapsed. His wife had only a minor wound and had remained in the suite at Sparrow Hospital with her husband through the night. A tube had been inserted in the governor's chest. He was expected to have a full recovery after a hospital stay of one to two weeks.

The would-be assassin, identified as Paul Sikes, was not an employee of the Kellogg Center. He had apparently walked into the building unnoticed in his chef gear. Previously, he had been a cook at other local restaurants; in each case, he was let go for possible addictive behavior. His first two wives had divorced him for the same reason. There was a restraining order to keep him away from a girlfriend and her two children from a prior relationship.

The gun he had used was a stolen Glock 42 .380. Police had not determined where he had acquired it.

Sikes claimed he was acting on orders from higher up, to save Michigan from a foreign conspiracy. He would or could not name the person or persons who gave him the orders. Police could not determine if this was the fantasy of an obviously disturbed man or if he was actually associated with a domestic terror group. They promised a thorough investigation by both state and local police and, because there were unverified rumors of a possible connection to the Boykin administration, the FBI.

A large crowd of well-wishers had gathered outside the hospital through the night. Some placed flowers near the entrance. Some carried signs such as "NITH NOW!" and "Change the Game"—slogans that became chants.

Almost every story in the *Journal's* front section made mention of the successful news conference leading up to the Kellogg Center celebration and, ultimately, the assassination attempt. One story, probably originally scheduled to be the lead article of the day, focused totally on the press conference—but it was relegated to an inside page. It was positive in its reporting on the work of NITH and the governor's strong support.

The lead editorial, while emphasizing the sorrow and anger, along with the prayers and well wishes of the editors and citizenry, urged lawmakers and the people at large to get behind the NITH effort, an effort, it said, to which Governor Birnbaum had not only dedicated his political career and reputation but had "almost sacrificed his very life."

Angelo folded the paper hastily and chose to forgo his usual second cup of coffee. He called Lana's room from the lobby. Realizing too late that it was barely 7:00 a.m., he apologized for waking her.

"So, you didn't sleep much either," she said. "I spent most of the night in the hospital with him."

Angelo heard the strain in her voice.

"He was doing much better when I left," she said. "Quite a scare."

Angelo said, abruptly, "We have to act now, Lana. For his sake, we can't wait for his recovery. We have to keep things moving, now more than ever."

"That's a good thought, Angelo. What do you have in mind?"

"We can't wait another month to get NITH together again. We need to move faster. We need to show action and we need to do it while the iron's hot."

"The iron's hot?"

"Well, damn it, mine is—and I think the whole NITH team probably feels that way. Maybe the public too, with all this happening."

"It sounds so callous, like we might be seen as exploiting the governor's injury. But, on the other hand, you may be right. The politics could be on our side for a short time."

"Exactly what I was thinking. But you know way more than I do about that."

"So, what do you propose?"

"I want to hold a session this coming weekend—up in my part of the state, in the Leelanau Peninsula. It would do us all some good to get away, almost like being on our own island. It's April, it's springtime, most of the snow is gone, and it's in between seasons. It's quiet. I'm sure we could find a place on short notice. It would be a great setting for reaching agreement on an amendment or two. We could take something concrete to the governor."

"I like it. Let me think about it. I'll get to work on arranging a space and getting the word out."

"We can do this."

"Angelo, I'm going to ask you right now. Will you take the lead at the meeting? You have become the man the whole group trusts. And, let me tell you, you have made me feel a lot better already this morning." Lana hung up without waiting for him to accept her nomination.

Angelo calculated that Lexi would be awake and wondering where he was, probably worried. When he let himself in the room and closed the door quietly behind him, he saw she was up and moving. She seemed a little put out with him.

"You didn't even leave a note. With all that happened last night, I have been worried sick about what was going on and where you were."

"I couldn't sleep and went down for an early breakfast." He filled her in on what he had read in the paper and about his conversation with Lana.

"A meeting in Leelanau," she said. "That's a wonderful idea." She tossed her suitcase on the bed. "We have to get back home then. We have to make some plans. I'm still mad at you. But I'm proud of you too. I'm sure Governor Birnbaum would be grateful."

CHAPTER 29

Homestead Evening

NITH met the next weekend on the Leelanau Peninsula, the "Little Finger" of the Michigan mitten. The Homestead Resort was not far from Angelo and Lexi's home in Eagletown, nor was it far from their beloved Sleeping Bear. People began arriving mid-day on Friday. Drinks were scheduled for five-thirty, with dinner and a short meeting to follow.

Since it was only a week removed from the night of the assassination attempt, the happy hour was less happy than normal. A few people were missing due to the short notice but most were there and others had said they would make it in time for the Saturday morning meeting.

Most of the conversation Angelo heard was about the events of the last week: the governor continued to improve, there were more rumors of conspiracies, and even possible terrorist connections. Nothing of any substance had been confirmed. As far as anybody knew, the shooting was another instance of a lone wolf trying in his perverted way to make some sort of statement that even he didn't understand.

As a result of the shooting, NITH had become more

visible. It had been in the news every day. Feedback was pouring in, most of it encouraging them to move forward on their early ideas. Editorials in many newspapers appealed for the public's support of Governor Birnbaum and his courageous and unflinching effort to fulfill his campaign promise to change the game. Of course, this only added to the group's determination to make something good happen.

Interspersed among those two major topics, Angelo was pleased to hear mention of the beauty of Northern Michigan, especially from those who had never been to this part of the state before. Perry Karas commented that the Red Wings preseason training camp always took place in nearby Traverse City in early September, a getaway that the players always enjoyed.

When they all sat down for dinner, Lana stood to welcome everyone and assure them of the governor's progress. Angelo felt embarrassed when she went on. "I also want to thank Angelo RoundSky," she said, "for setting things up on such short notice. Our meeting up here, in this beautiful part of the state, was all his idea. Just now, over drinks, I've been hearing a lot of people rededicating themselves to the success of our mission. That was Angelo's purpose in suggesting this get together. He was—as most all of us were, I'm sure—sad, angry, and determined when things all started to sink in.

"I'm sure it upset some plans and schedules for all of you to be here, but I'm also sure that this is where we *should* be this weekend. As I have promised before, I am not going to interfere with your deliberations, but I felt as determined as the rest of you to be here, where the action is."

Angelo stood, sensing it was his turn to speak. "Lana, we need you to speak when you want to speak, say what you want to say, just like everyone else here. As someone said at our last meeting, 'we need more voices and more choices.' Also, I want to say that I'll have a little announcement when we finish eating, so please don't anyone leave until then."

As the group dug into their food, the conversation topics remained as they were before dinner but with a bit more vigor. Some were gratified to observe Angelo's newfound assertiveness and commented on their curiosity about his announcement. All expressed their growing respect for the man.

When dishes were cleared and napkins put aside, Angelo rose again and people rang their spoons against their glasses. He spoke in his usual modulated tone and cadence.

"Instead of a regular start for our meeting tonight, Lexi and I arranged a little trip. (He wanted to say 'my wife, Lexi and I,' but they weren't quite there yet.) We are blessed to have a perfect evening for it. For those not already dressed in casual clothes, I suggest you go to your rooms and change. Put on something you can get around in outdoors. It will be chilly. We will meet in front of the lodge in fifteen minutes, where you will find a bus waiting."

The mood turned more lighthearted as people, full of curiosity, boarded the bus for the short trip through Glen Arbor, into the National Seashore area, past the climbing dune, and onto Pierce Stocking Drive, the road that wound its way up to the top of the Sleeping Bear. Lexi was waiting for them and led them up the short walkway to the dune's edge, while Angelo brought up the rear.

Murmurs moved through the group as they took in the spectacular view out over the inland sea of Lake Michigan and then looked down the steep 450-foot cliff of glacial sand running down to the water's edge. Named "the most beautiful place in America in 2011 by ABC's *Good Morning, America*, it was, indeed, breathtaking.

When they had all gathered, Angelo spoke. "This is our spot, Lexi and me. We thought if you came up here and took in all this beauty, and, stretched to see as far as you could see over that great expanse of freshwater—maybe all the way to Wisconsin—if we did this together, we might all see the immensity and the beauty of our lives on this planet, and see beyond our differences to those things we all have in common: our common purpose as a group, including protecting all of this and making lives better for all our citizens, for seven generations to come."

He paused to let them take in the panorama. The sun was already setting and the few pink-shaded clouds promised a glorious sunset.

"In the peak of summer," Angelo said, "the light in the western sky hangs on until after ten o'clock. We can't, as mortals, stop time or other things that happen beyond our control, as we have recently been reminded. Although the days are getting longer, our time to get our work done is getting shorter. We had planned on months to complete our work, but things happened beyond our control. Now we need to work as though the sun is about to set. Take it all in tonight. Enjoy it. Be mindful. And then we will get down to work tomorrow morning at eight."

His words were followed by a silence as meaningful as the scene before them. He and Lexi embraced and turned to the north toward the Manitous. As the sun lowered over the pink and blue waves of the inland sea, the evening's ambient light took on a peach glow. Then the orange sphere, having traveled far to the south but now on its way back north in its journey, began to find its way to the horizon, sending out rays to the postcard-perfect clouds, slashes of purple and red appeared against a deep-blue backdrop. A chill began to climb up hundreds of feet from the sandy shore below.

It was a quiet ride back to the resort but not a somber one. A copy of the Sleeping Bear Legend had been placed in each room.

CHAPTER 30

Homestead Weekend

Angelo was happy to see everyone seated in the conference room early the next morning. There were books and papers in front of each of them, he guessed put there by Lana. He sensed common purpose and positive momentum tempered only by the challenge before them. In addition to the many public suggestions, everyone was well aware of substantive differences of opinion within their membership. Despite the assassination attempt, and despite the awe-filled evening they shared atop the dune, those differences were still there. Angelo opened the meeting by asking Lana if she had any news from the governor.

She smiled and said, "I do. First, let me tell you that letters and texts and emails of support for our governor and for the work of this group have been pouring in. Even from my lovable, hardcore-conservative grandfather. There has also been a significant increase of support from our state officers and our legislators, some who we assumed were our opponents. Governor Birnbaum spoke of changing the frame at the press conference—how if you change the frame, you change the whole picture. Despite the awful events of last week, they have changed the frame. So, more power to us and pray that we are up to the job. As for the condition of my friend, the governor, I'm glad to report that Charlie is out of the woods and on his way to a full recovery. He will have a tube in his lung for a while. He needs rest, but this morning he was awake and feeling well enough to send this text:

Victor Hugo: "Armies cannot stop an idea whose time has come."

Our time is now. Carry on your courageous work.

This time there *was* applause, wholehearted applause.

"So let's *do* this, my friends!" Lana said. "Based on the output from your last meeting, we have given each of you three books—*Future Perfect* by Steven Johnson, which discusses peer networks and many other ideas you talked about; *Citizenville* by Gavin Newsom, which talks about 'more voices and more choices,' and other topics; and *Happy City* by Charles Montgomery, which was cited in your presentation. In addition, there are some interesting papers covering the pros and cons of sortition, or selecting a legislature by lot, and of a unicameral versus a bicameral legislature. Thank you to Tom Samuels and Perry Karas for bringing some of these papers to my attention. I have been digging into them myself. Stimulating."

Nodding toward the woman seated next to her, Lana added, "Speaking of resources, there's Joss. She may be a newcomer for some of you, but I think several of you know Joss by now. She is not only my dearest friend, soulmate, and the love of my life—she is also the managing partner of one of the top law firms in the state.

This weekend, as we move toward drafting one or more amendments, she and I can help you with the legal requirements involved in that process."

Joss smiled and said, "I'm looking forward to working with this group. Besides what I read in the papers and on the internet about all the good work you're doing, Lana also filled me in on your progress. I know that sometimes lawyers are seen as the people who tell you *no* so as to keep you out of trouble. Not this weekend. I am here to help you find a way to say *yes*—but in such a way to bypass any legal barriers."

Angelo spoke up. "Joss, thank you for being here. We're rookies at this and need all the help we can get. Lana, we need you too. Don't hold back. Lem, you're our moderator."

"Not if I can help it," Lem Tracker replied. "Seriously, I would rather not. I don't want to stay above the fray. I want to be able to express my thoughts and feelings. As moderator, I can't do that. You have been doing fine, Angelo. Why don't you stay in the lead?" His suggestion was followed by several hear-hears.

"You've done such a good job, Lem, thank you. I've never been a moderator," Angelo said, "and what if *I* want to say what's on *my* mind?"

Cher Richie responded. "Then *do* it. We need to hear you. Hopefully we've matured some as a group since our first morning session in Flint." She rolled her eyes before going on. "Wow, doesn't that seem longer than two weeks ago now? Anyway, let's just start in and let the chips fall where they may. If we find we need a moderator later, we can always switch. Lana, you jump in if you think we need help. Last time we broke into subgroups but I think we should first try as a whole to move on from where we left off. We can break up later if we think it will help. In my opinion, the biggest overriding issue—and maybe the most contentious—is the fundamental lack of trust in our state government. Perry addressed that in his 'Imagine' presentation. I boil it down to two main ideas: sortition and transparency. In the interest of restoring trust, I think those are the two concrete, actionable proposals. Madeline and Tom thought we should just offer some tweaks. And that's where we left it."

Wayne Keith said, "What about the other issues we discussed in the other groups—things like education and the environment, and health and safety?"

"So important, Wayne," said Cher, "but we're up against the gun here." She stopped herself. "Oh, dear, unfortunate word choice. I'm sorry but if we're going to come to some form of agreement on one or two amendments over this weekend, those other issues, while important, might be too much. We need to narrow our focus, not try to cover everything. If we just address trust in government in one or two amendments, those others issues can and will be addressed by the new state government."

Angelo said, "I get what you're saying, but the environment is near and dear to me. Wayne and Martha care the same way about public education. We talked about a Bill of Responsibilities. Can't we at least make a statement in a more general amendment along those lines?"

"Like an amended preamble," suggested Susan Kerns.

"I like that idea," said Cher. "We *should* say something about inclusiveness and, of course, the economy. Those all affect the trust issue too. Maybe we can address multiple issues in a preamble."

Tom Samuels spoke up. "I think that's good. Let's do

it, but first things first, like picking our legislators by lot."
He chuckled.

Angelo looked down at the table. He sensed Tom was
picking a fight. Perry just smiled and said, "I know where
you stand on that one."

Samuels paused for a second and then said, "I know
I took the other side before, but things have happened
and I've been doing a lot of thinking. And studying. In
fact, I've already read some of the items Lana brought for
us this morning. Wynn, you'll be pleased to know that I
actually read about peer networks in *Future Perfect*. Look,
I still believe in a chain of command. I still think we need
clear leadership. But last Friday night was a life-chang-
ing event for all of us, I believe. I know it was for me.
Governor Birnbaum is our leader. He is the reason we
are even here talking about this. When I think of what
happened—I mean, I looked him in the eyes up close
while I was still holding that guy's gun. I saw a look I will
never forget. Sure there was shock and pain—but I also
saw a fierce look. He was not just scared, he was mad and
determined. I always liked the governor, even though I
often didn't agree with him. He's a fun guy, a charmer.
But this man was and still is dead serious about changing
our state and our state government. On this mission, he's
my commander and he wants this. What he has said all
along finally sunk in: he won't be satisfied with incremental change. He's committed to something much bigger
than that. He's my commander and I'm a good soldier.

"And, as I have thought more and studied more, he's
right. Our system really is broken, and we can't just
tinker a little with it. It's not just one or two problems,
it's a whole, big, complicated mess. We need to deal with

the *whole* mess as one big mess, not fix a problem here and there. We need a whole new game. I'm convinced of that now. I'm ready to listen. So, Perry, let's go over those things you said we should imagine one more time."

"Well, that just leaves me, doesn't it?" said Madeline Edges. "I'm still leery of jumping off a cliff. Maybe that's because I watched my business collapse. But Tom's right, the governor chartered our group to create something transformative, not to tweak what we have. Ever since our first meeting in Flint, I have been trying to decide if I can get on board with those expectations. If not, I thought I should just resign from the group. But the more I thought about it, the more I began to reflect on my own life and career. If you will allow me, I would like to take a few minutes to tell you about some of my own experiences."

She related the story of how she and her husband met at Great Expectations, an old used bookstore on an Ann Arbor side street, when they were both undergraduate English majors at U of M. It was the sixties, the time of SDS and sometimes violent protest on the Ann Arbor campus—but reading and talking about books and ideas with each other and their friends was the way they expressed their rebellion. When the owner, who had become a friend of the group, retired, he offered the store to them at a very low price, and they scraped enough together to buy it.

"Over time, we began to sell new books, even best-sellers, and, in addition to the old-book lovers who were our regulars, we began to get all kinds of people into the store. We did what we could to exploit the charm of the old place and it began to make money—and boy, did we need money. Being successful also meant having more customers and making more money. We used the money and a big loan to buy a large vacant store location right on the edge of campus, but we didn't call it Great Expectations, we called it Edges. That was the first Edges bookstore—and the rest is history, I guess. When my husband died, I became the CEO. I was determined to show that I could do it on my own, without a man."

She described how she forgot the basic ingredient to their success: choosing book lovers like themselves to run the branch stores and leaving them alone while taking advantage of the economies of scale of a chain. "There were real threats to the book business at the time. Without even realizing it, I began to become more of a micromanager. As I have been sitting out there in Chelsea these last few weeks, loving books again, I woke up to how much I had changed and how I managed and what effect that had on the branches and the good people who ran them. I may just be able to *imagine* again, Perry. It feels good to start something up again instead of closing it down. It felt scary when John and I went into debt for Great Expectations. It feels good to be a little scared again, to use my imagination again, to have great expectations again. Mostly it feels good."

Perry broke the silence. "Maddie, you are amazing for telling us that story. I knew a little about your company's background but I know so much more now, and it means so much more. We all have our own stories to tell. Thank you for sharing yours. I'm sure you have much experience we could learn from."

"I will share one other thing right now," she responded. "Call it a cautionary tale. As a woman who gave birth to two children and as a woman who went through a long struggle starting up a business and the long, heart-breaking loss of that business, I tell you now, without reservation: giving birth is difficult but resurrection is a miracle."

That provoked some laughter. But Angelo, a Native American whose people had suffered over a century of genocide, and now about to become a father himself, felt the truth in her words.

Wynn, who had been leaning back in his chair as he listened to Tom and Maddie, sat up straight. "Now you have me *really* scared. I was prepared to deal with disagreement this weekend. But now, I don't know. Now I have to be more careful what I wish for, don't I?"

"What we're telling you and Perry and the rest of you," said Tom, "is keep doing what you did to get us here. I'm still a practical guy—an engineer who likes to see a blueprint—not so good at dreaming. We have the bare bones. Now, let's put some meat on them. What do all those 'Imagines' look like in the real world? We need the specs.

"I think you told us that these ideas are already being practiced somewhere in the world right now and that they are working. What would they look like in our state, in our constitution? We may have come around to a new way of thinking but we have a long way to go in translating that into action."

Perry replied, "Like Wynn said, be careful what you wish for. Now we have to move past inspiration and get down to the nitty-gritty. We have a couple lawyers and a new state Representative to help us."

Susan Kerns brightened at the reference to her and spoke. "Right, but while we're telling stories, Perry, you have told us of your strong belief in true democracy. As a newly elected state House member, I'm curious. I'd like us to start there."

"Well, since my middle-school disillusionment with the McLaren Cup and Councilman McLaren's pompous pronouncement that we had a republic and not a democracy, I have made it my business to study the history of democracies all over the world, from ancient times until now. When I tossed the idea of sortition out there, knowing it would be controversial, I was not ready to throw myself on any swords over it. Now that we have talked more about it and, like Tom, now that I have studied some of the things that Lana brought us this morning, I am convinced of the merits of the whole principle. I know it still seems like a radical idea, but I'm ready to be an advocate."

CHAPTER 31

The Blog

NITH

Percy Oliver, Names in the Hat/
Michigan constitutional Council

Posted on April 6, 2019

Good Morning, Michigan.

Once again, I am Percy Oliver,
your NITH blogger, bringing you
up to date regarding our progress on amending the state constitution of Michigan. For a complete account of today's session,
please see our podcast. This blog
is just a summary.

After an inspiring trip last evening to take in the view from the
Sleeping Bear Dunes, you could
sense the group's quiet intensity
this morning. Once at work, we

surprised ourselves with the effi-
ciency with which we moved through
the task before us. This is not to
say we didn't sometimes engage in
vigorous debate. We did. We had to
deal with difficult issues to which
there are no easy answers.

People spoke their minds openly
and listened with open minds—at
least as open as the minds of
people with strong views can be.
Many people commented that the
momentum and cohesiveness seemed
to have soared in the aftermath of
the attempted assassination of our
leader, Governor Birnbaum.

Summary of Proposals
[Note: Jocelyn Urabana, Managing
Partner, Urabana Associates, was
in attendance. She and Lana Hartman will be working with members
of NITH to draft the final, legal
language of two amendments based
on our proposals below.]

The Stewardship Amendment
In our previous meetings, we discussed adding a Bill of Responsibilities to balance our long-hon-
ored US Bill of Rights, which is
already acknowledged in our state
constitution. This addition will
address our need for stewardship

of our environment (especially
our precious lakes and rivers};
for the education of our children
and youth (and even opportunities
for continuous learning throughout
life—true cradle-to-grave community education); for an economy to
create and support jobs and quality of life for our citizens; for
public health and safety; and, over
it all, responsibility for creating and sustaining a climate of
trust between government and the
citizenry. We came to call this our
"Stewardship Amendment." It was
suggested that the oath for all
legislators include a pledge to
stewardship.

The Governance Structure Amendment
Benjamin Franklin said, "Congress
should be a mirror of the people."
John Adams wrote that a legislature
should be "in miniature, an exact
portrait of the people at large."

In fact, our present Congress is
mostly male, mostly white, mostly
rich, mostly college-educated.
"The people" it supposedly represents are 50% male, 30% college-educated, and 5% million-
aires. This says nothing of the
lack of ethnic or racial diversity, or the fact that lawyers are

227

over-represented by a very large
margin. In other words, Congress
is far from any resemblance to a
"portrait" of the people. The same
can be said of our state legislature. We are governed by a political class that is very different from the citizenry. Numerous
polls show Congress with a lower
approval rating than used-car
salesmen and the bubonic plague.
Using some form of random selection, on the other hand, Congress
would come much closer statisti-
cally to a "portrait in miniature." About half would be female;
two thirds non-college graduates;
and ethnic, racial, and economic
groups would roughly approximate
their presence in the country as
a whole. Importantly, given this
diversity, they would be much more
likely to represent the thoughts
and values of the people as a
whole rather than a particular
political party or special-interest group. For those concerned
about the potential for lack of
competence in legislators selected
at random, extensive research
has shown that diversity trumps
ability. We are committed to the
notion that we need "more voices
and more choices."

Therefore, we propose: A randomly selected, nonpartisan unicameral legislature (with appropriate legal restrictions and exemptions) of 150 representatives. Peer networks may be sanctioned by the legislature as appropriate and may be initiated by office holders or citizens themselves. Legislators shall be limited to two three-year terms, staggered so as to have experienced cohorts in office at all times. Complete transparency will help assure accountability of legislators and empower citizen participation in governing, while greatly reducing time and money now spent on campaigns and elections.

Conclusion
Further detail of our rationale for these proposals can be found by viewing our podcast of the proceedings. You are encouraged to do so.

We left our meeting with a kind of somber satisfaction, perhaps exhausted from wrestling with vitally important but difficult issues, but happy and committed to the results while at the same time subdued at the realization that we may not meet again with these people we have worked with so closely. This may be my last blog on the subject. But maybe not. Who knows?

Tags: NITH, Live Streaming, Sorti-tion, Random Selection, Michigan Legislature, Unicameral, Political Parties, Peer-to-Peer Networks, Stewardship

What do you think?
We are eager to hear from you and will respect all points of view provided they are offered in a respectful manner. Rude troll comments will be deleted from this site.

Enter comments here

CHAPTER 32

Ceremonious Occasions

After lunch at the Homestead, Angelo, Perry, Julia, Lana, and Joss made their way back up to Sleeping Bear. Angelo was smiling. "It's an eagle feather," he explained when he sensed their surprise. In addition to the feather in his braided hair, he was also wearing a clean white shirt trimmed in Ojibwe symbols. The plan was for a simple civil marriage ceremony presided over by Joss, but Lexi wanted a few traditional Native touches. "A little something for my mother and your grandmother," she told him.

As they waited at the top of the dune, Angelo, the nervous groom, calmed himself when once again he took in the view. "When I look out across the lake," he told the others, "I always say I'm looking for Wisconsin. It's more than that. To me, the western horizon and beyond are the future, but I'm also looking to the past. They say this dune, the Mother Bear, and her cubs, those two islands to the north, started out in Wisconsin. Ojibwe believe that all time is a circle. From up here, I try to sense the whole of the circle. Sometimes I almost can."

They heard a faint but steady drumbeat from the direction of the parking lot below. It slowly grew closer.

Finally, two older female drummers in ceremonial attire came into view, Lexi's mother and Angelo's grandmother. A glowing Lexi followed close behind. She was striking in a long, white wedding gown adorned with Ojibwe icons. *Two* eagle feathers were held in place in the back of her head by a turquoise-beaded headband that encircled her shimmering black hair.

With Perry and Julia as best man and bridesmaid, Joss presided over the civil service. At the moment of the ring exchange, Grandma Emma stood before the couple and spoke briefly in her Native tongue, then translated: "To feel true mutual love is to know and love the *Gichi-manidoo,* the Great Mystery, because the very breath of *Gichi-mani-doo* is considered the giver of human life. It is through love of oneself that we express our love for the Great Mystery of Life. *Migizi*, the Bald Eagle, represents the teaching of love because he flies high above the earth and is therefore closer to the Great Mystery than any other creature. Love is the most elusive of all virtues and no other creature is so elusive as this mighty spirit-bird, and love has the same light and airy nature as his feathers."

Angelo and Lexi exchanged rings of white gold, engraved with eagle symbols. After he kissed the bride, Angelo beamed at her before he looked out at the natural beauty of the sand cliff, the backdrop of lake and the sky. For him, the simplicity of the ceremony came layered with his memories, dreams, hopes, and aspirations.

The small caravan moved on to the newlyweds' Eagle-town neighborhood for a ceremony they were keeping under wraps. Having put off knowing the sex of their baby, now that they were married, Lexi and Angelo decided they could wait no longer. They would make the two happy announcements on the same day.

Neighbors and friends had gathered in the cul-de-sac outside their home and on the vacant lot next door, enjoying a keg of beer and some snacks. The wedding party arrived a bit later than planned, and people were well into the party mood and restless in anticipation of the main event. A mix of cheers and boos met Angelo and company as they emerged from their cars and exchanged handshakes and hugs with the small crowd. Loud music vibrated from a boombox.

Angelo's old friend from school days, Frank Crowley, pulled a hockey stick from the back of his pickup and handed it to Angelo. Crowley held three pucks and invited Perry and Lana to join him and Angelo into the street.

Days before, Lexi and Angelo had asked her OB/GYN to place a paper with the baby's sex in an envelope and then, blindfolded so they wouldn't see, the doctor helped them Skype Frank Crowley. They then opened the envelope just enough for him to see the paper before they burned it. He was the only one to know.

Crowley took the stick from Angelo, handed it to Lana, and got ready to drop a puck. Lana was ready and made solid contact sending the disc down the middle of the road. Next was Perry, who took his best slapshot and sent the puck whistling two feet off the ground until it landed well past Lana's before running several more feet on the pavement. The crowd let loose with their own whistles of appreciation.

Angelo took his position, ready to outdo his friends. Crowley dropped the puck. Angelo connected solidly as the puck then burst into thousands of tiny flakes of blue powder.

Everyone was taken by surprise, no one more than Angelo, his hockey stick dropping to the concrete. The silent detonation discombobulated him for several seconds before it began to dawn on him that he was soon to become the father of a boy, leaving him even more stunned.

It was some time before the other interested spectators could take it in as well. Lexi ran to throw her arms around the boy's father-to-be. The two held each other until their faces broke into shocked amazement and then hysterical laughter.

"It's a boy," shouted Crowley, anticlimactically, and the spectators erupted in cheers and applause. Perry and Lana cracked up and rushed to hug the soon-to-be parents. The entire wedding party then joined the celebration in the middle of the street.

The happy couple made the rounds of friends and neighbors, getting hugs from all. Finally, Angelo asked Crowley to whistle his loud, shrill whistle because he wanted to make an announcement. With Lexi beaming at his side, Angelo said, "First of all, Lex and I want to thank all of you for coming out for this reveal party. As you can imagine, it's been an exciting time for us ... and our little boy. Just before we came over here, Lex finally made an honest man of me. For about the fourth time, she asked me to marry her and I finally gave in. We are now man and wife, as well as soon-to-be proud parents of a little boy. So, thanks, everyone. Let's keep the party going."

CHAPTER 33

The Power of NITH

It was only two weeks after the wedding when Lexi picked up Angelo's vibrating phone and checked the caller ID before handing it to him. "Guess who?" she said. He looked at her quizzically as he put the phone to his ear and she mouthed the name Lana Hartman.

"Back to work," she said. "But first, how's the bride coming along?"

"All three of us are doing great, thank you."

"As you might imagine, it's a very busy time."

"Politics."

"Listen, Angelo, I have a big ask ..."

"Anything I can do."

Angelo smiled at Lexi as she stopped emptying the dishwasher and went to the bedroom. He knew she would be listening in to the call.

"I hope you mean that. Joss is working the legal side of things and the governor, his staff, and I are all working the politics. More important than any of that, though, we need to rally public support so the professional politicians can't stop us. They need to hear from the voters."

"You know way more about that than I do. So how can I help?"

"I remember the stories you told about the way the Algonkians governed themselves."

"*Some* Algonkians," he emphasized. "That was a long time ago."

"Okay, but what about the "battle chief" or "war chief" or something like that?"

"Battle chief. It was a temporary job," he said. "After the battle, he was made to go through a rite to rid himself of his temporary power. He had to wash it off."

"That's the one. We need you to be our battle chief this summer. We don't have much time left to get on the ballot for the August primary. You're going to lead our statewide campaign to drum up popular support. I've watched you grow into a natural leader with NITH. For a while, you never said much, but when you did, people hung on your words—they respected you and trusted what you had to say. Then, as you became more involved and revealed more of your background and character, you became the man."

"I was just doing what I thought was right. I wasn't going to let anything get in our way."

"And that's precisely what we need now, someone who won't let anything get in our way."

"I don't know anything about public relations campaigns. I would need help with the technicalities. Plus, I'm stuck way up here in Northern Michigan."

"Don't worry about the technical stuff. We have professionals who can help you. As for downstate, you can recruit from NITH."

"Cher Richie and Wynn Stewbie are down in the

Detroit area. They are both good with digital stuff. They would come in handy with a social media campaign."

"It sounds like you're accepting the job."

"The temporary job. Then I'll have to get it all washed off me."

"Understood."

"We're going to need advertising too, and video. And budget. Cash."

"See how much you know already? We'll help get you whatever you need to go into battle."

"I need to say the usual stuff—how humbled and flattered I am—because frankly, I am. And more than a little nervous about it. But excited too. I hope I can measure up."

"I have no doubt on that score. So, tell me, you've been married all of a week or so—how's married life treating you?"

"Like I said, we're all doing great, but you may have just cut into the honeymoon."

"Oh, dear, what were you planning?"

Angelo laughed and said, "I'm just kidding. Our only plan was to stick around here and do our thing. We do live in God's country, you know. And it's peak season up here. Why go anywhere else?"

"Well, now you may have to get around and see the state."

"Right. Could be fun, but I'm taking my baby momma with me."

"As you should, my friend. I wish the both of you all the happiness in the world. Please tell Lexi I said so. I'll be in touch."

Lexi strolled into the bedroom, a smirk on her face. "Battle chief, huh? Well, what do you know about *that*?" Lexi said.

"What about *you*, Lex?"

"What *about* me?"

"I'm thinking two things. One, you've been in that management job at the cherry co-op for some time now. You're good at it. And two, you were at Standing Rock."

"So?"

"You told me how well organized the protest was there. The logistics. The way different groups worked together and all that."

"It was amazing. I still find it inspiring."

"So, why don't you take charge of that part of our campaign?"

"That's *your* job. And I'm pregnant, remember?"

"You would be better at that job than I would and we need the best people on every job. I think you could pull this off."

"I'll have to think about it. You caught me by surprise."

"This whole thing catches me by surprise."

They were interrupted when Angelo's phone rang again. Cher's name appeared. "Hey, partner, what do you think?" he asked, assuming she had already talked with Lana.

"It will be great to work with you; that's what I think. I'm looking forward to it, partner."

"We're going to need social media. I'm depending on you."

"Working on it already, Angelo. I'll have some ideas to run by you soon."

"We can't do all this with just the two of us. We need to round up a band of warriors."

"Right," she said. "Of course. I've got millions of people to cover down here and you've probably got that many acres."

"And trees, don't forget to count the trees," he laughed.

"Especially in the UP," she said.

"Right. I'm going to start by contacting Nick Lahti. I also have another guy in mind, not a guy from NITH."

"No need to limit ourselves to NITH members, although we should use them where we can."

"Have you ever done a PR campaign?" Angelo asked.

"Not me. You?"

"Nope. So, here we go again. Amateurs running the show."

"As it should be," Cher said. Look at where the so-called pros have gotten us. 'All the people,' remember?"

"And I'm good with that. But we need to do this together. We don't have much time before the we're on the ballot for the August primary."

"Let's do it. Stay in touch, Angelo."

"Just Ang is good, Cher."

Next Angelo called Lahti in Houghton and filled him in, asking him to be on the team. "We're going to need some help up there, and I have at least one other guy in mind. Do you happen to know the Garfield Township Police Captain in Mackinac County?"

"That's a long way from Houghton," Lahti said.

"Of course, just thought maybe. His name is Dan Jankowski. I dealt with him on the Enbridge Line 5 thing a couple of years ago. We were on opposite sides but he's not a bad guy and I think he's popular among the locals. I'm going to give him a call, if that's all right."

"What the hell? You're the chief, right?

"Enough of that chief business, Nick. I'll be in touch. We'll need a conference call soon."

Next he looked for the business card Jankowski had given him in the Engadine days and punched in the captain's office number. A man's voice answered. "Captain Clark's office." Jankowski, it turned out, was retired, replaced by Clark. Angelo explained who he was and asked the dispatcher to pass his number onto the retired captain.

Within the hour, Angelo got the call. "Dan Jankowski here. So what the hell do *you* want?"

"I thought you were probably out fishing."

"The fish are having a quiet day. Then I hear from Clark's office there's a bad-tempered Indian fella comin' after me. Thought I'd better head him off at the pass. How you doin, eh? Never thought I'd ever hear from you again."

"Captain, I need you."

"A little late to admit that, ain't it?"

"Way too late."

"So, what's up?"

Angelo filled him in on the back story of the constitution project and his role in it as best he could.

Jankowski said, "Yeah, I've been reading about that and seeing stuff on TV. It's definitely time for some big changes in our government. The two parties just going after each other, the usual bullshit. And then the guy in the White House is a dangerous nutcase. I voted for Charlie Birnbaum because of all that nonsense, and he seems to be trying to do the right things. Awful shame about the assassination attempt. You were there, I read. From what I've seen, he's coming along okay."

"He needs you now. That's why I'm calling."

"He needs *me*?"

"Well, I need you on his behalf. You know people up there and they like you. They voted for you many times over the years. Something tells me you know how to mount a campaign directed to the folks in that part of the UP."

"Maybe, maybe not."

"We have another good man in Houghton and I know a woman in Escanaba I'm planning to ask."

"Just tell me what you want me to do. Fish ain't bitin' anyway, and it might be nice to feel useful again."

Angelo and Cher Richie enlisted Wynn Stewbie, which took care of the multimedia piece. They decided to use a crowdsourcing site to raise money beyond what Governor Birnbaum and Lana could come up with. The extra money would help with the finances, while also raising awareness and commitment from people. Percy Oliver would continue to blog and use his MSU contacts.

When Angelo asked Lana and Percy to recruit students to work the campuses and neighborhoods, thousands of enthusiastic young people hit the streets. The amendment campaign required a minimum of 300,000 legal signatures; which, in reality, meant many more were needed to get past any possible legal irregularities. The students were trained by a professional petition group hired by Lana, but the actual drive was carried out by the volunteers. Soon they were going door-to-door for signatures and mounting public demonstrations of support in a variety of ways. Students, workers, and sports and entertainment celebrities joined arms and marched together in communities across the state.

Cher and Wynn launched a powerful strategy using Facebook, Twitter, and Instagram. Other sites, such as change.org for online petitions, amplified their influence.

Angelo worked with the governor's PR staff and an ad agency—but he also had another idea. The Traverse City Film Festival always included Native American entries, and Angelo knew and respected the work of award-winning documentary filmmaker Gwen Katherine, whom he persuaded, with little resistance on her part, to make both short- and long-form television ads.

The various opponents, as Lana had predicted, pulled out the stops as well. The campaign was hit from both the right and the left. Dark money generously provided for their opposition's campaigns. Lobby groups, that would no longer be able to finance campaigns for or against a candidate, were threatened by their potential loss of influence, and fought back hard. The NRA was doubly challenged by the reaction to the attempted assassination of Governor Birnbaum and the possible lessening of its financial influence by a random selection of lawmakers. It went deep into its substantial war chest to fight the amendment. Fake news stories appeared on Facebook, reporting false scandals about many of the NITH members and Lana and Joss's relationship. Lawsuits were filed that challenged the legality of the amendment and petition-signing processes. Joss's law firm and the governor's lawyers handled those cases independent of Angelo's warriors but he stayed in the information loop in all cases.

The opponents' campaign emphasized the risks of the proposed new form of government, the need for experienced leaders, the loss of that great American privilege of voting, and of jumping off into the unknown. They did their well-funded best to exploit the fear factor.

It didn't hurt at all—in fact, it might have provided a significant turning point in the campaign's favor—when Boykin finally woke up to the impact all this might have on him and his November Presidential election chances, which were already looking pretty dismal. His early-morning Tweet — *Michigan heading toward catastro-*

phe. Birnbaum off his rocker. Lunatics running the asylum. I can fix it — produced an immediate and widespread backlash in the state. Even Senator Billings flinched and called the governor privately. "Charlie, I can't take any more of the Boy King. I'm still a Republican but I admire what you're trying to do, even if don't totally understand it. You can count on my support."

Meanwhile, Gwen Katherine's ads focused on the need to change the system. She used Birnbaum's favorite metaphor as a running tagline: "It's not enough to change the players. It's time to change the game." As people became familiar with the concept, the tagline was shortened to "Time to Change the Game," which became the motto for the ads and the entire campaign.

Opponents attempted to counter with the slogan "Government Is NOT a Game"—but it never acquired traction.

Katherine also created an hour-long film that opened with a scene of the turbid waters of the Flint River with a swirling fade into a montage of the perils of the existing system, the watery swirl from Flint a recurring backdrop for live footage from the floor of the Legislative bodies at both the state and federal levels that showed representatives from both parties making self-righteous proclamations based solely on partisan politics; political campaigns that demonstrated even greater schisms; town hall meetings with outraged citizens from all political polarities clamoring to be heard by their indifferent and defensive representatives; and clips of those citizens complaining that they were not being heard. Continuing the film's dizzying spiral, President Billy Boykin made multiple appearances with outlandish Tweets superimposed on his brief scenes; as did Senate Majority Leader Richard

McShay of Tennessee and his use of the so-called nuclear option to cut off debate on a Supreme Court nominee; and a prominent pundit's comment that McShay had just killed the Senate itself.

Following brief but effective use of charts and data from the Michigan Fractured Trust study, the montage concluded with the Flint River rushing like a tsunami up and over the Michigan Statehouse building itself, finally fading to the famous scene from the movie *Network*, when news anchor Howard Beale urges citizens to "get up right now, sit up, go to your windows, open them and yell—'I'm mad as hell and I'm not going to take it anymore.'"

The film then shifted to the renewal mode, with clips from the Michigan Speaks Conference and the NITH meetings, showing grassroots citizen participation and lists of their values, goals, and concerns; eventually focusing on the positive points of the proposed amendments. Portions of interviews with NITH members and other supporters were shown, including an endorsement from popular columnist Jimmy Owens. The movie concluded with cellphone video of the assassination attempt on Governor Charlie Birnbaum; mugshots of his alleged assassin; and, finally, Governor Birnbaum recuperating in his hospital bed, making a strong plea for supporting the need for a new way of governing. The governor was obviously not at full strength but his charisma managed to shine through as he made a passionate argument for not just fixing a few problems but for fundamental change of the underlying system. "Time to change the game," he said.

The film ran as a documentary in the Traverse City

Film Festival not long before voting day. Some NITH members, including Angelo and Lexi, appeared in person after the film for a Q & A session.

Thousands of citizens provided feedback and suggestions on the crowdsourcing site, all of which were considered in the final proposed amendments. Cher Richie and Wynn Stewbie digitally combed through the names of these contributors and, in consultation with Angelo, drafted many of them into joining the battle.

Meanwhile, on the political front, Lana and Governor Birnbaum worked the elected officials, as well as the shakers and movers from local governments, and leaders in the private sector-state and federal legislators and their key staff, mayors, union leaders, and the CEOs of prominent Michigan companies. Lana and Charlie sought out supporters from all segments of the state power structure, the gatekeepers and opinion leaders. They did their best to include everyone of influence, but when they knew they were fighting a losing battle with an individual or group, they backed off and henceforth treated them with what might be called "benign neglect." Instead they focused their energy on the supportive forces: prodded and roused and stirred, urged, inspired, shocked, and spurred; lighting fires in, with, and around them.

They assembled supporters into action groups. They didn't just take one approach, but instead came at these leaders from multiple directions and with multiple appeals. They enlisted the help of the innovators and opinion leaders who had emerged from Michigan Speaks.

They individualized and attempted to find the currency, metaphorically speaking, of each VIP. Lana kept Birnbaum informed of her activities out on the trail while he worked the phones from his home as he continued to recover. It became a symbol of prestige to be seen visiting with the recovering governor. In other words, Lana and Charlie got as much leverage from playing the sympathy card as they could.

Sometimes it seemed like one step forward and two steps back, but they bobbed and weaved like the pros they were, pressing the issue and then backing off, surrounding the resisters with supporters, fluidly moving with the situation. They were changing the big picture by changing the little ones.

As voting day approached, Jimmy Owens' column appeared in the *Detroit Free Press*:

> Drums Along the Grand
>
> Time is growing short, and perhaps the most impressive manifestation of the spirit of this movement toward a new democracy in our state has been the crowdsourcing. And I'm not just talking about the financing. I mean crowds, baby, all kinds of crowds.
>
> Biggest, most-impressive crowd of them all? The Water Protectors, led by quiet, modest, courageous Native American mother-to-be, Lexi Pullman–RoundSky, from Eagletown, a small reservation community up in beautiful Lee-lanau County.
>
> Who would have thought that after the amazing phenomenon that was Standing Rock was pushed off the headlines, such a happening would ever occur

again? But there they were, the Water Protectors—people from throughout the Great Lakes Region, including Canada's First Peoples and their allies, mostly from Ontario; and others from the so-called Seven Nations—all camping out along the Grand River in Lansing and on the banks of the Red Cedar at MSU, flowing to the Capitol during the day and even to Grand River Avenue here in Detroit.

It is Michigan's Water Wonderland that brings them here—our inland lakes and streams, and the Great ones—Ontario, Erie, Huron, Michigan, Superior. It is the threats of Enbridge 5 to these Great Lakes; of Nestlé to our groundwater supply; and of clean drinking water to the people of Flint, a city still under a siege brought on by the previous governor. Water brings these protectors together; and their hope and belief that a real democracy, worthy of trust, can help save our natural resources.

Of course, there has been blowback about "outsiders," but the overwhelming strength of support is undeniable.

These actions have evoked not only memories of Standing Rock, but also reverberations of our own pots-and-pans revolution of only a few years ago that brought down the state House/Stenhouse gang and, in some ways, gave rise to Charlie Birnbaum and the democracy movement itself. Except this time, the people aren't banging wooden spoons on kitchenware, they are drumming away on Native ceremonial drums; sometimes joined by drum corps from high schools and colleges operating "out of school" so to speak, risking their status with their institutions.

Together, these groups collected over 400,000 signatures—without paying a dime—almost unheard of in the history of petition drives in this state. "It shows the enthusiasm of everyday people wanting to make sure this change happens," said Pullman-RoundSky. Drum, drum, drum. Ratta-tat-tat.

Military veterans showed up in force too, as they did at Standing Rock. "We fought for the right to vote," some vets complained, but most veterans at these rallies answered in overwhelming numbers that their military service was not about voting or not voting but for democracy and freedom and a government of, for, and by the people; a government worthy of trust; a government worthy of fighting for. So, they drummed too. Rat-a-tat-tat.

I see that I am typing the word *overwhelming* a lot. But that's just what it is. All of it. Drum, drum, drum. In a constant, consistent, persistent rhythm. Drum, drum, drum. Ratta-tat-tat. All day and well into the night (everybody has to sleep some time), they drum and they dance. Peacefully, always peacefully, though not without resistance from protesters on the other side. But peacefully toward the protesters and respectfully to all.

And—to the frustration of their opponents' legal challenges—lawfully.

Drum, drum, drum. Rat-a-tat-tat.

Drum roll: Time to vote!

CHAPTER 34

Michigan Speaks: The Vote

On the morning of voting day, the breaking news was not the proposed amendments to the constitution but that Paul Sikes, the would-be assassin of Governor Birnbaum, was found dead in his cell of an apparent suicide. Although officials promised a thorough investigation, it had already been determined that he was a lone wolf, having lived a life of petty crime, chronic addictions, and multiple disappointments. There were, however, calls for programs and policies to improve mental health care, Governor Birnbaum the face of that effort. Gun control regulations were on the table.

As for the vote itself, an unusually large turnout was expected for an August primary. Lana and the governor were confident. Not Angelo. Lexi was proud of her work. She was deeply grateful and inspired by the passion of the Water Protectors. Nevertheless, as always, she sensed her husband's feelings and did her best to cheer him up.

At eight that morning, they went to vote. Outside the voting area, they chatted and took in the encouraging words from their Eagletown friends and neighbors.

By mid morning, Lexi, after watching Angelo pace

and scroll through television channels watching the same news over and over, suggested a drive around M-22, the scenic highway circling the Leelanau Peninsula. It was a hot, hazy late summer day, past the July tourism peak, with many families having to return downstate to prepare for the start of school. Nevertheless it was still a busy time up north.

They had coffee at a diner in Northport and then slowly made their way to Leland for lunch, where they managed to get a table at the popular Bluebird Cafe. After lunch, they strolled down to the Fishtown harbor area where they enjoyed ice cream cones and took in the clear view of the Manitous. As Lexi suspected, the sight gave Angelo's spirits a lift. They both knew where their next stop would be.

As they looked across Lake Michigan from atop Sleeping Bear, Angelo said, "Ya know, whatever happens with today's vote, I'm content. We did all we could. You especially. Whatever happens, we will still have each other and soon baby Mark—and this view. We will always have this."

"For all time, Ang," Lexi said as she wrapped his arm firmly around her side.

"For all time, Lex. Let's spend the afternoon down at Empire and North Bar Lake."

They had a long standing tradition of swimming in that shallow lake every month of the year at least once, but not this day. Instead they walked along their favorite Lake Michigan beach, looking for good skipping stones. Even though he felt some sympathy for his wife's condition, Angelo could not let her win the skipping contests along the way. When Lexi pleaded for a short break, they stopped at a favorite resting place, a huge, flat, turtle-shaped rock. It was nestled in the dune grass where they sat down to watch the gentle waves lap at the sand.

After a bit, Angelo stood and aimed his phone camera at the mother-to-be. She laughed at him and stood on the rock to pose herself in profile, a mock glamour pose that purposely emphasized her swollen belly. Just then, another beach stroller came along and offered to take their picture together.

Angelo handed the man his phone and stood beside his wife on the rock. Neither had any trouble smiling.

They then walked back into the town of Empire for dinner at Joe's Tavern. It was just five-thirty.

There was still plenty of daylight as they retraced their route on M-22, taking them back into Eagletown and home.

After the polls closed at 8:00 p.m., virtually all eyes in the state of Michigan were glued to televisions to take in the results of the vote. Charlie Birnbaum, his wife Jacquie, and their guests, Lana and Joss, were in the living room of the Governor's Mansion in Lansing.

When it was announced at 11:30 p.m. that both amendments had passed with more than 70% of the vote from an unusually large turnout, Charlie Birnbaum opened a bottle of champagne against the advice of his doctors. A series of toasts moved from him to the others, beginning with words of heartfelt gratitude that soon plummeted into jokes and laughter.

He couldn't thank Lana enough, repeating his praise for all her work. His effusiveness finally made her laugh. "Charlie," she said, "I don't know which I feel more—joy or relief. It's been an exciting ride, but now I'll be glad to get back to teaching law."

Birnbaum's smiling face turned sober. "What do you mean, teaching? I only have two years left in my term to get all this stuff implemented. A new game, remember? The people have handed us the opportunity to transform the political landscape of our State, maybe even the country. As Maddie Edge said, 'we're not giving birth here, we're attempting a resurrection, a miracle.' You and I have a deadline, not a choice. You can't quit now."

Joss laughed at Lana's stunned expression.

For the moment, Lana could only sigh and down her glass of champagne.

In Eagletown, fireworks and shotguns could be heard going off. Angelo's phone rang almost the moment the results were announced on TV. It was Perry Karas. "Hey, Ang, what do you think about that?"

"Great, man! Just great! What are you guys up to?"

"We're at my parents' house—me, Julia, and Lamarcus. Julia's folks are here too, joining right in with our big Greek-style celebration. Lamarcus has been cracking everyone up. My Grandma Achima is still awake, way past her bedtime, dancing, drinking retsina. I'm worried about how she's going to feel in the morning! We're all just having a blast. How about you? How's Momma Lexi coming along?"

"Momma Lexi is just fine. We're having a little celebration here, too, with my grandmother and Lexi's mom. My guess is our party is quieter than yours, but we're all happy."

"Hey, man, we owe you and Lexi a bunch for pulling this whole thing off. You're the first people I thought of when I heard the results. Thank you so much, man.

"You too, Perry. You did a lot, you and Julia. Enjoy the party."

When they hung up, Lexi said, "I'm glad Julia's parents were there."

Angelo's and Lexi's phones continued to chime. They finally turned them off and gave contented goodbye hugs to grandmother and mother. When they were alone, they sat quietly on the couch, with the sound muted on the television, holding each other, feeling the baby kick, dampness in their eyes.

After a long silence, Lexi said, "Wow, Ang."

"Yeah, I know," said Angelo. "We won *this* battle."

"What do you mean *this* one?"

"I have a feeling there will a few more. Big ones." He paused and smiled. "But right now, I think we need to cleanse ourselves of *this* battle . Let's get in the shower."

They both laughed through their tears.

ACKNOWLEDGMENTS

This book, like any other worthwhile project, is the result of collaboration. I want to thank all those who worked with me in this attempt at creating something meaningful.

I have been interested in the contrast between white and native American views of power since my graduate school days when I read "Two Concepts of Authority" by Walter B. Miller, but it was a former master's degree student of my own, Angie Shinos, who helped me with details of everyday contemporary native life back when I was just starting to write this novel. In the late nineties, Merrelyn Emery, an Australian social scientist/consultant, first introduced me to the concept of sortition, another idea that I couldn't shake until it found its way into this book. My son Chris, Associate Professor of Interactive Multimedia at The College of New Jersey, led me to the work of one of his former NYU graduate school professors, Steven Johnson, whose book *Future Perfect* makes a strong case for peer networks as an organizing principle.

Once I had woven these and other ideas into the first draft of a story, I needed the help of two strong editors to whip it into shape. I asked the gifted essayist, Rick Bailey (*American English-Italian Chocolate* and soon to be published *The Enjoy Agenda*), to be the beta reader of my early efforts, and, as a generous favor, he came up with a skilled line-by-line edit. When it was time to move to publication, Mary Jo Zazueta applied her considerable professional talents to the final draft. I am also indebted to the pros at Mission Point Press for guiding me through the maze of publication, especially Bob Deck for his work on the book design and Doug Weaver for sharing his overall experience and wisdom.

Finally, I need to thank Pennie, "wife, lover and mother of my baby." Her years of love and patience even extended to the time I spent on this work.

CPSIA information can be obtained
at www.ICGtesting.com
Printed in the USA
FSHW01n0544080818
51082FS

9 781943 995776